The
SEC
D0427375

ALSO BY LILY GRAHAM

The Summer Escape
A Cornish Christmas
Summer at Seafall Cottage
Christmas at Hope Cottage
The Island Villa

The Paris SECRET

Lily Graham

Published by Bookouture in 2018

An imprint of StoryFire Ltd.
Carmelite House
50 Victoria Embankment
London EC4Y 0DZ

www.bookouture.com

ISBN: 978-1-78681-628-3
eBook ISBN: 978-1-78681-627-6

For Mom and Dad, with love

CHAPTER ONE

The old woman on the train didn't look like the kind of person who had a secret burning darkly, deep inside her chest. The kind of secret that twisted itself around the heart, squeezed tighter than a fist, ready to burst.

But she did.

One that, if she only dared whisper it aloud, would cause more than a few of the strangers around her to gasp, even now, after all these years.

Strangers who might never have imagined such a thing hiding behind the worn face of the woman sitting by the rain-lashed window, clasping a burgundy cashmere shawl to her neck, her fingers red and gnarled and painful in the sudden snap of cold weather.

The young don't think about the old that way. They don't see the scars time has left behind, the heartache, the joy. They only see the blank face of old age.

Certainly, the young woman with dark hair, tired eyes and a bulging laptop bag bouncing against her hip, who'd offered to help stow the old woman's suitcase in the luggage rack overhead, didn't stop to think of her in that sense. If she thought of her at all, it was merely as someone in need of a helping hand, perhaps, or someone less likely to object to her taking the available seat next to her, where she planned to go over her notes for the talk she would be giving the following day, in relative peace. Vowing as she did every week that it was time to look for a different job.

The old woman's suitcase was cobalt blue and old-fashioned, the kind covered in stickers of faraway places. The young woman swung her glossy hair over her shoulder, setting her teeth while she hefted the suitcase into the available space above their heads, using an elbow for traction as it began to slip, almost regretting her offer of help when the suitcase nearly came crashing down on her head. She muttered a curse, and then cleared her throat when the old woman looked at her with a frown, making an awkward attempt to get up and help. 'I've got it, don't worry,' she said, forcing a smile.

At last she heaved the case up, wedging it between a large tin of chocolates and a grey duffel bag, and sat down, blowing out her cheeks, which had grown pink from the exertion. 'That was heavier than it looked – don't tell me you're fleeing with the last of the Romanov jewels?'

The old woman's green eyes brightened. 'Just my memories. They are heavier the older one gets. Particularly when you frame them.'

The young woman laughed, showing very even, white teeth.

Around them people were still boarding the train from Moscow, glasses fogging in the sudden warmth of the interior, wheeling suitcases behind them, their faces showing the spectrum of excitement and resignation that marked most travellers facing a long train journey ahead of them, with this one coming to its end in Paris.

A recorded voice came over the loudspeaker, announcing that the train would be departing in the next few minutes.

The young woman settled into her seat, then rubbed her neck, a casualty of the brick-like pillows at the drab hotel they'd put her up in near the Moscow office. She opened her laptop and took out her headphones, which she was planning to use to drown out any distractions while she concentrated on her work; but then she frowned, curious despite her better intentions, as she considered the old woman's words, and turned back to her, a question on her lips. 'You travel with your photographs?'

The woman nodded, and a loose strand of powdery white hair slipped out of the chignon at the nape of her neck, which she tucked behind an ear, her hand shaking slightly. Her nails were filed into rounded ovals, the colour of pearl. There was a faint trace of perfume, floral, pleasant and expensive.

'I like to keep the people I have loved close to me, wherever I go.'

Whatever flippant remark the young woman had intended – along the lines of a suggestion that the old woman consider going digital in future – died before they could leave her mouth, as the older woman's words touched something inside: the barren pain of missing someone you may never see again, all too real since her mother had passed away two years before. She sucked her bottom lip, as if to tuck the emotion back in, and said instead, 'I can understand that – home wherever you go, that's… lovely.'

The old woman nodded. 'It's not quite the same as the real thing, though. I suppose that's why I'm going back to Paris now, after all these years. I can't quite believe it myself.'

The young woman detected the trace of an accent, English mixed with something else, possibly French. 'Home is in Paris?' she asked. 'I'm Annie, by the way.'

'Valerie,' said the old woman, with the kind of smile that transformed some faces, showing the young person hiding beneath the passage of time. Then she answered Annie's question. 'Yes, Paris is home, I suppose. Though I've spent most of my life away from it. I've been travelling these past few years now, since my husband died. I always wanted to see Russia, and thought, well, why not now? Though I went all over first. Prague, Istanbul, Morocco… but yes, Paris is always home when I think of it. Funny how that works, isn't it?'

Annie shrugged a shoulder. 'I've never lived anywhere else, so home for me is always a little house in the Kentish countryside. Makes it easier, I guess, when it's all you've ever known. I can't imagine actually living in Paris, it seems incredible to me. Baguettes any time you want, croissants, cafes spilling onto cobbled streets, the fashion…' She sighed, eyes alight picturing the romance of living in the City of Light – and love. 'I've always wanted to find the courage to move there. Maybe one day…'

The old woman nodded. 'I couldn't imagine living there either when I was around your age, when I moved there by myself. I was terrified, actually, and I didn't feel like I could ever fit in – I wasn't exactly fashionable. I was an assistant librarian… alas, to the core, clunky brogues and corduroys, mostly.'

Annie grinned. 'That's fashionable now – nerdy chic?'

Valerie chuckled, a throaty sort of laugh that belied her age.

'So what made you decide to move to Paris then?' asked Annie.

The old woman's fingers played with a signet ring on her left hand.

'I wanted to know who my family were, rather desperately, and that need was stronger than the fear, in the end.'

The train started to move, and the station whooshed past in a grey and blue blur, from men and women scurrying to their destinations, to the sudden shock of green and gold of the countryside. An announcement came over the loudspeaker that refreshments were available in the middle carriage, with a selection of hot and cold meals.

Annie was dying to hear more, but she saw Valerie look towards the back and guessed, 'Coffee? I can get us both some.'

'That would be lovely,' said Valerie, opening her purse and handing her a note. 'Black, please. My treat.'

'Thanks very much,' said Annie.

As Annie navigated her way past people's elbows and knees, in desperate need of a caffeine fix, Valerie thought about the past. How could she not, when that's what this trip was about after all? She'd finally be back where it had all started, where her whole life had changed, after all these years.

There was a part of her that couldn't help feeling the same trepidation she'd felt as a young woman when she'd first made a trip, similar to this, over forty years before. She twisted the ring again, a garish thing made of brass and bad taste, a nervous habit she couldn't break.

Annie came back, handing her a Styrofoam cup filled with steaming black coffee, just as she'd asked, then looked at the ring Valerie had been twisting, but didn't comment.

Seeing where Annie's gaze had fallen, Valerie gave a small, wry shrug. 'It was my grandfather's, once upon a time, it's horrid really, but I love it all the same because it was his,' she said with a small hollow laugh, taking a sip of the coffee.

Annie closed her laptop and sipped her coffee too. She was curious about the woman sitting next to her, despite her good intentions to go over her work – she was diverting, to say the least. She'd always had a fascination with people and their stories; sometimes she couldn't help herself, like now.

'You said earlier that the reason you went to Paris was to meet your family? They were French?'

Valerie nodded. 'We were separated by the Second World War, when I was just a child. I was taken to live with a distant relative in England – I was told that it was for my safety. I was never reunited with my real family, not until well after I was a grown woman.'

'I'm sorry,' said Annie, who couldn't imagine how awful that must have been.

Valerie shrugged. 'Just another casualty of war, I suppose. What so many men have failed to realise after waging all these wars is that there are no real victors in the end, not really – there are only casualties, and they keep coming long after the battle has passed. I was in my twenties when I found out that my family were still alive. Well, one member was anyway.'

'You didn't know?' gasped Annie.

'I had no idea. I was told they were dead. I was raised by my mother's cousin. For the purposes of avoiding too much confusion, I was told to call her "Aunt Amélie". She'd married an Englishman during the war, my uncle John, and I went to live with them. I was told that there was no one else alive, after my mother died, apart from Amélie. When I turned twenty, she felt that I deserved to know the truth. It is only now that I am old that perhaps I have begun to understand why they did what they did. How they thought that the lie would spare me the pain.'

Valerie sighed sadly.

'For some, the truth is a burden. Something that can never be restored once unleashed – a Pandora's box – but for me it was the opposite. It was an anchor to the past, providing me with a sense of belonging, even if it was a painful one to bear.'

Annie put her headphones down. Discarding them next to her laptop, she had a feeling then that she wouldn't be opening it for the remainder of the journey.

'So you decided to go to Paris to find your family? To find out why it had been kept a secret that they were still alive?'

Valerie nodded. 'It was 1962, and though it's been many years now, I can still remember where I was sitting when I boarded the train from Calais. I didn't have the window seat then,' she said with a small laugh. 'There was snow in the air, and all I could hear were Amélie's words going through my head. *Don't do it, Valerie. Don't do this, please.* But I had to.'

'She didn't want you to go and find them – even after she told you about them?' asked Annie with a frown. 'Why?'

Valerie twisted the ring. 'It was more that she didn't want me to be disappointed – I'd been given up, after all. She didn't want me to expect some fairy-tale reunion. Didn't want me to open a wound that might never close. But I wasn't after the fairy tale. Just the truth. I had to find out why they did what they did. Why they had sent me to a strange country to be raised by someone else – a stranger, really, even if we were distantly related.'

The train sped along, and Annie was swept along with it by the old woman's words, hurtling through the khaki and gold countryside, and into the past.

CHAPTER TWO

Paris, 1962

The whistle blew as the train slid into the station in a billow of fog and cold. Valerie craned her neck to see out of the window, past the woman seated next to her.

Paris.

She couldn't believe she was here, that she'd gone through with it in the end.

Well-heeled passengers stretched lazy limbs and put on the coats, scarves and hats they'd abandoned hours earlier in Calais.

An old woman muttered, '*Névé.*' Snow: she could smell it in the air.

Valerie shivered in her borrowed coat, though it was nerves more than cold that made her shake.

She was a slight figure, made more so by the heavy tweed coat that draped beyond her toes, shapeless as a tent, and still smelling of Freddy from when he'd slung it about her shoulders. She breathed it in, the mixture of aftershave and something that was always, somehow, home. Before she'd boarded the ferry, he'd put his head against her forehead, and said, 'You don't have to do this – you know that, right? We could have our own adventure here, just you and me?'

She'd nodded, a lump in her throat, because she had to go. If she didn't do it now, she never would.

Valerie closed her eyes. Thinking of Freddy wouldn't help now. Beneath the shapeless coat, she wore the thin, rose pink cardigan with the hole by the left elbow, and the faded pearl buttons that Aunt Amélie had sewn onto it when she was thirteen. She hadn't worried about its lack of style, till now.

She took down from the luggage hold her aunt's old suitcase, which was tied with string to keep it from bursting open. Across from her a woman, with a silk scarf expertly knotted at her throat, looked her up and down, seeming to bookend her worn cloak and clunky brown brogues with something akin to pity. Valerie looked away, touched the folded letter in her coat pocket, felt the sharp point of the envelope – which had turned into a softened round crease from her worrying fingers – and drew courage; *this* was why she was here. She hadn't had time to assemble something fashionable, not that she had the money for such things. Times had been tough lately.

She raised her chin slightly, then opened up her suitcase, slipped off the coat and put on an extra jumper, and wound a hand-knitted scarf around her neck. If there was snow, then she would be prepared for it. Even if she wasn't prepared for anything else.

He'd sent a map, along with the letter. It was thoughtful of him to do it; later she'd realise just how out of character it was too. Though it stabbed her heart a little to think that the closest living blood relative she had would need to send a map for her to find him.

Still, after today, they would be reunited. That was what mattered most.

The job would help. She was luckier than most. Besides, the advertisement had said that no experience was necessary, just a love for books. Well, that was her, wasn't it? As a trained librarian and former bookseller, Valerie had escaped into books the way some women escaped into the arms of men: headfirst, and without a life jacket.

Amélie's words rung in her head, even now. 'But Valerie. This isn't like a story from one of your books. I'm not sure how he will react when he finds out. Vincent Dupont has always been a mercurial man. He may not respond in the way you hope, when he finds out that you've come.'

It didn't matter, not really, thought Valerie. Besides, people who didn't read thought all stories were fairy tales. They weren't. The right ones taught you about who you could be if you tried. If you only stepped outside what was comfortable, and safe, and known. The only thing she needed right now was to have courage.

As she walked out of the station, past the press of people, she caught her first sight of Paris, and she felt a stirring of joy, as if there were an effervescent bubble floating beneath her feet, making her step lighter and bolder, chasing away the fatigue of travel. Despite the cold, there was a golden tinge to the air, like the fizz of champagne, and it painted the buildings in an amber-pink glow.

The last time she'd been here, she was three years old, running through the streets with her aunt, on their way out of the city. If she closed her eyes she could almost remember it. The way her feet slapped the cobblestones, her aunt's troubled grey eyes, the pressure of her arm against hers, firm and relentless, even as Valerie whined that she was tired. As they raced, she could see in the distance a group of uniformed soldiers entering the street. Amélie paused, and Valerie walked into the back of her legs, then her aunt turned quickly, and told her to be quiet, that they needed to go another way. *Now.* When she hesitated, her arm was pulled roughly for her to follow. There were tears in Valerie's eyes, but she didn't cry out any more, she just did as Amélie told her. *Vite*. Hurry.

Valerie didn't know now if it was a memory, or if her brain had simply invented it after Amélie had told her, but it felt real.

She headed down Rue des Arbres, past buildings with statues cut into the facades, past cafes with tables that, even in the cold autumn sun, with its unseasonal snap of snow forecast, spilled onto the pavements, bringing with them the scent of freshly made *café noir* and baguettes, and the sound of people.

She headed for the area of Saint-Germain-des-Prés, the playground of artists and vagabonds, which had in recent years been reclaimed by writers and feminists, revolutionary thinkers, jazz hands and the melting pot of cultures.

Despite her map, all too soon she found herself lost, walking along the serpentine slither of the Seine, marvelling at all that she saw, despite the fact that she had no idea where she was. Forty-five minutes later she found the bookstore, tucked between a bistro and a flower shop, on the Rue des Oiseaux. It was called 'Gribouiller': scribble. A touch of whimsy that she would later find improbable at best or derisive at worst.

She hesitated at the thick wooden door, the colour of a duck's egg, peering in through the small window where the gold letters of the shop's name were etched, yet faded by time. She turned the brass knob, and the bell above the door tinkled.

Inside, a ribbon of light filtered from the window and fell on an old man with cotton wool for hair, who sat in the corner at a large mahogany desk crammed with books and letters and overflowing ashtrays. He was smoking a cigarette and didn't look up, just waved a thin hand, the middle fingers stained brown from his cigarettes. 'A franc for the new books, fifty centimes for the old. Take your time,' he said in a croaky voice.

Valerie hesitated, aware of the heavy sound her clunky brogues were making on the dusty wooden floor. She stopped as close to his desk as she dared, her eyes taking in the rows of custom white bookshelves and the helter-skelter piles of paperback towers that jockeyed for position over every available inch of the shop, her heart pounding now that she was here. Now that there was no turning back. 'Bonjour, M'sieur. I am here about the position.'

'Position?' he said with a frown, as he continued to stare at the ledger before him. Blinking his blue, rheumy eyes, he removed a pair of wire spectacles from his nose, placing them on top of the desk with a small, audible sigh, reluctant to be parted from his work.

'For the bookseller.'

The man looked up at last and leant back into his brown armchair. There was a rip on the side, exposing a bellyful of stuffing. He paused mid-drag on his cigarette, and peered at her through the blue-grey swirl of smoke with a frown, as if what he saw didn't seem to provide much clarity either.

'You are English,' he said after some time. Not a question but a mere statement of fact.

'Yes,' she answered. It couldn't be helped; her voice going slightly higher than she'd intended. She cleared her throat. 'I wrote to you a little while ago,' she said, attempting to prod his memory, her stomach plummeting with an unwelcome thought – had he *forgotten*? Taking out the letter from her coat pocket with shaking fingers, she was about to hand it over. It wasn't older than a week but it had been twisted and bent and read so many times, it felt like a part of her.

The old man frowned, and put back on the pair of wire-rimmed spectacles he'd abandoned earlier. Then he got out of his seat with a grunt, and shuffled forward to look at Valerie properly. What he saw didn't seem to impress; she'd taken off her coat, displaying two jumpers and a long brown velvet skirt, and by her thick-soled shoes sat her much-battered suitcase.

The old man seemed to frown deeper at her long golden-blonde hair and green eyes for a moment more, then at last he gave the slightest hint of a nod, though he made no move to take the letter.

'You're the girl, the scholar,' he said with a sniff, though his blue eyes seemed slightly less cool than before, Valerie thought. But this may well have been a trick of the light. He clicked his cigarette-stained fingers, as if to jolt his mind into remembrance and a small mountain of ash hit the floor by her shoes, leaving a peppery sprinkle on their polished surface. 'The – the one with that – that paper.'

'"The challenges of bookselling during the war: a study of two cities during the Blitz and the Occupation",' Valerie quoted. 'Yes. I am Val—' She paused, then quickly corrected herself, speaking louder: 'Isabelle Henry.' She gave the false name, hoping he hadn't noticed the error. They spoke in French; she knew that he wouldn't have it any other way. She had been warned by Amélie.

'Vincent Dupont,' he said, looking at her extended hand briefly with a raised grey brow, his lips emitting a small 'pfft' sound. She removed her hand quickly and smiled awkwardly.

She stared at him, taking in everything from his white hair to his long nose, which bulged slightly at the tip, to his sharp, impossibly pale blue eyes, his stooped back, tan slacks and loafers, and the emerald cardigan with leather patches on the elbows, where a book with a pale yellow dog-eared cover sat against his hip, half buried in the left pocket.

He gave a small nod. 'I will show you to your room – it's nothing much,' he warned, leading her to a flight of stairs behind his desk, which led to the upstairs apartment and the small room she would be using, which, according to the advertisement, had a single bed, a sink and a kettle. The latter, she was to assume, was the *pièce de résistance* in the pursuit of luxury accommodation. Tea and sugar were not included. Monsieur Dupont was not running a charity. She didn't mind. She was here at last, that was all that mattered.

Her heart skipped for a moment as she followed him. The stairs were tiled in black and white, and spiralled like a turret shell, and she found to her surprise that she recognised them, could picture herself in a pair of red shoes that sparkled in the sun, playing a hopping game on them as a little girl. She let out a low gasp at the sudden, forgotten memory.

A memory of here. She held out a hand to the wall to steady herself, noting as she did that the walls had changed – they used to be white, but were grey now and peeling, in need of fresh paint. There used to be a brass railing but that was gone now too, replaced with a cheap plastic barrier.

Not understanding her moment of shock and surprise, the dawning realisation that she had been here before, Monsieur Dupont swivelled around to look at her, his vivid blue eyes, which were rimmed red all around, narrowing. 'You're not going to change your mind now, are you? I had it cleaned. I explained that you'll have a small room in the apartment above the shop – I never made it sound like the George Cinq in that letter, I'm sure,' he said, his tone weary, impatient.

She shook her head fast, and clutched her suitcase with white knuckles, giving him what Freddy called her megawatt smile. 'Oh no, it's perfectly fine, thank you, it's wonderful.'

He looked at her a little oddly for her overzealous enthusiasm. 'You haven't seen it yet.'

She coloured slightly.

He turned the brass knob and let her into a small apartment, which was flooded with light that fell onto a polished wood floor in a herringbone pattern. There were wide windows that looked towards the streets of Paris, with the Eiffel Tower in the far distance. Opposite the living room was a kitchen, with a round table and a small shelf housing a thin stack of ageing cookbooks.

He showed her the bathroom, then led the way to a tiny room on the opposite end of the apartment. He unlocked the door, and pushed it open with a bit of force. Inside the air smelt musty and disused. There was a single bed covered in a patchwork quilt, a child's wardrobe, a tiny sink in the corner which was slightly rusted, and on a low stool at the end of the bed, by a sliver of a window, sat the infamous kettle, with a mug and a teaspoon. She could touch both sides of the walls if she held her arms out. 'It's good, *merci*,' she told him.

He made a noise of assent. 'I'll let you unpack before we start work. The shop is open six days a week, with a break for lunch from two, then back at work at from five till nine. Will that be a problem?'

She shook her head.

He nodded and turned to leave, then cocked his head, staring at her with a frown, and she wondered if perhaps for a moment he recognised her at last. But then he said, 'Fish?'

'Fish?'

'You eat it?'

She nodded. And he left, saying, '*Bon*, dinner.'

She sat on the bed after he had gone, trying to slow her heart rate as she unwound her thick woollen scarf from her neck, looking around at the little room.

He hadn't recognised her. There had been a moment when she'd held her breath, thought that he would have realised who she was, seen something familiar in her eyes, her smile. But he hadn't.

She took a deep breath, berating herself for her romantic notions. He hadn't seen her in seventeen years, and it wasn't as if she'd given him her real name. She suspected now that if she had, there was every chance that Aunt Amélie was right: that he *would have* thrown her out.

CHAPTER THREE

Three weeks earlier

London

The advertisement for the post of bookseller at the Gribouiller was a tiny sliver of a thing, wedged in next to an ad for a position at a jam factory in Lyon, and another for a couturier in Montmartre, and measured just three lines. But to Valerie, it may as well have been written in block capitals on the front page; the name of the bookstore had leapt out at her and stopped her heart.

Freddy had taken it from her, placing the paper on the somewhat sticky wooden table inside their favourite corner pub that always smelt like stale cider and Scotch eggs. 'Don't,' he'd warned.

She'd looked up, her green eyes meeting his dark brown ones. Hers had that look. A look he recognised, and he groaned. 'I *knew* I should have kept this to myself.'

He'd found the advertisement by accident in a week-old copy of *Le Monde*. He wished now that he hadn't shown it to her.

She'd given a reluctant grin, despite the fact that everything seemed to be falling off its axis as a result of seeing the ad. 'You wouldn't have dared.'

He'd put his head in his hands, making his wild brown hair even more dishevelled than usual. Freddy had the sort of boyish looks that would follow him till the end of his days. It was what made him such a good journalist: no one took him seriously until it was too late. 'No,' he admitted. Freddy was the first to admit that where Valerie was concerned, getting perspective was an unachievable goal.

She'd downed the rest of his warm beer, pulled a face, then stood up, giving him a salute as she made to leave the warmth of the pub. 'I've got to get some air, think about this,' she'd said, barely ten minutes after they'd sat down.

Freddy had stared after her in confusion. 'Well, I'll see you later then, yeah?'

She'd nodded absently. All she could think of was the words from the advertisement, which reverberated in her skull like the beating of a drum: bookshop assistant required, must love reading, no experience necessary, room available with *kettle*.

It had seemed like a sign. A way in.

She'd left the pub in a daze, and walked the streets of north London in the rain. She spent that evening drafting the letter, telling her grandfather everything but the truth – her interest in French literature, her love of reading, her longing to spend a year abroad, the opportunity such a post would give her for completing her education, and the fictional paper she was writing about bookselling during the Second World War. Appealing to his French pride, by stating that she was sure that it had been more difficult during the Blitz than the Occupation… something told her, from what Aunt Amélie had explained of his temperament, that this might help ensure that she at least got a reply, even if it was simply a scathing one. She'd decide what to do if he said no later.

She'd be asking a lot, she'd written, if he could take her on without interviewing her first, as the trip to Paris would be such a high cost for her on her assistant's salary from the British Library. She suggested that she could work for free the first week as a trial, offering to do the cooking in exchange for the room and information about the shop during the war, and the return fare home if the arrangement didn't work out.

She'd waited impatiently for a week and half for a reply, haunting the letterbox every evening as soon as she was home from work, but every day there was nothing and she'd begun to lose all hope.

Freddy had turned his big, brown eyes on her incredulously when she'd told him what she'd done. 'Oh, Val, you silly sod,' he'd said, giving her a hug. 'A trial? Did you honestly think he would have gone for that?'

She'd closed her eyes and leant into his tweed-covered arm, feeling like an idiot. Freddy always told her she was living in a dream world. It was what he liked most about her, though – her eternal optimism, the way she saw the world as it could be, and never how it truly was at times. It often meant, though, that the fallout was that much worse. He'd been around enough times in the past to pick up the pieces, as her best friend and next-door neighbour.

She'd been in love with Freddy Lea-Sparrow since she could remember, from the first day her Aunt Amélie had introduced her to her neighbour, with his unruly mop of brown hair, tanned face and laughing brown eyes, and it was a habit that she'd never quite broken, even though being several years older than her she'd had to watch broken-hearted every time he had some new girl on the scene, which had been often enough growing up.

There hadn't been many of those recently, not since his job as a journalist for *The Times* had become so demanding – there wasn't much time for a love life when you were out chasing a story.

Now, though, at his words, Valerie had felt as if a stone were descending in her stomach. Wryly, she'd wondered if it were the weight of her own stupidity, sinking in.

Of course her grandfather wouldn't give some unknown English bookseller a trial, and let her move into his apartment: who would?

Why go to all that effort when he could simply hire someone who lived in the city, someone he could simply kick out that day if it didn't work out? Someone who wasn't asking so much of him.

Which was why she couldn't believe it when she opened the door to the flat that evening and saw the letter waiting for her in the letter cage. She snatched it up and opened it fast.

23 September 1962
Mlle Isabelle,

With some trepidation, I agree to your terms. I would like to say that it is a suitable arrangement but I have learnt that one should never state things one might regret in writing. If nothing else I look forward, in the way one does encountering a rabid dog, to meeting the sort of mind that imagines bookselling during a few bombings would be less congenial than during the Nazi Occupation of Paris. Consider my offer of temporary employment, then, a patriotic duty.

I must warn you, however: as to the position in question, my standards are exacting. They are French standards, which you will not be used to – coming from a nation with so few standards to set any stock by. As a result, I do not foresee that you will last long. However, I have been persuaded to be magnanimous as I have yet to find suitable staff in the city, so it is possible that a miracle could occur and we could be agreeable to one another, but I have as much faith in miracles as I do in English cuisine. I must warn you, also: the hours are long and the pay is below minimum wage. If this is acceptable I am pleased to provide a room (with a kettle). I must stress that I cannot allow you to do, as you suggest, 'the cooking'. I am an old man, who has endured enough in his life, and will not risk

English 'cuisine' in the winter of my years; I am certain my constitution could not bear it. If this is agreeable, I will see you next week at your convenience. I have enclosed a map.
Sincerely,
Vincent Dupont

Which was how, on a cold Tuesday, Valerie had handed in her notice at the British Library, and went home to tell her aunt and uncle that she was moving to Paris the following week, to find her grandfather – to their shock and dismay. Valerie knew that if she showed them the letter or told them about her plan to work for him in secret this would only have made them worry more. But it was Freddy, really, who had the most objections.

'You can't just go.'

'Why not?'

His eyes widened. 'What if he's crazy? He sounds crazy. And arrogant, and a bit mean, Val. What if he throws you out when he finds out who you are? You won't have any money to your name and you'll be stranded in Paris. I just don't think it's a good idea.'

She stared at him, the brown eyes she'd loved for most of her life, his unruly mop of hair. She'd do anything for Freddy, but not this. She couldn't stay, not now that she had the chance to finally meet her grandfather! To find out about her mother, her parents. 'I have to go – don't you see? It was a sign.'

'It was just an advertisement.'

'That *you* found, Freddy.'

He pulled a face. 'Don't remind me.'

She touched his arm. 'I'll be all right.'

He sighed. 'I can see that you see it that way – as a sign – but why don't you do this sensibly? You can't just run over there by yourself…'

'Why not?'

'Because it could all backfire. He gave you away for a reason, Val. I know that you want this fairy-tale reunion but I'm just not sure you're going to get it.'

His words were harsh – they were similar to the same objections Amélie had given her the day before – and Valerie's eyes smarted when he said them. It was more important than some imagined fairy tale. Why couldn't they understand that?

'I'm not going there so that we can have a big reunion, or to replace who I have. I love my aunt and uncle, my life in London. This is for *me*. I want answers, Freddy, I want to know what they have kept from me my whole life, and why. You just don't get it.'

Freddy didn't understand, and he never would. His parents had lived on Simmonds Street in north London his whole life. He was a London lad born and bred, along with the rest of his family, who all lived not far from his doorstep. The furthest relatives he had lived in Edinburgh, and that was as varied as it got. He knew everything there was to know about himself, and his family. He belonged. Valerie was a foreigner. A girl who had a faint accent even now from her early years in her aunt's care, where they spoke more French than English. As a result, despite the fact that England was the only country she really knew, when she went to school, and made friends, she was always marked out somehow as the French girl, yet she knew nothing except the bare basics of where she really came from.

It was a topic that she was never encouraged to broach. 'That's in the past,' Amélie would say; whenever Valerie mentioned Paris, her mother or the war, it was the same. The only stories Amélie shared with her about her mother were ones of her as a little girl. It never occurred to Valerie that it was because she hadn't really known her to be able to tell her more. Valerie would only find that out much later, when the truth would raise more questions than she had answers for – about why she had been sent to live with someone who was for all intents and purposes a *stranger*.

Some days she felt English, she truly did, despite her lack of English blood. Her bookish bent, her friends, her interests were English and it was home now, yet occasionally there were those little moments when it just wasn't: when the lie came crashing down around her ears, when she heard French music, or the sound of a woman's voice, and something tugged and choked at her heart, making her picture Maman. A woman she'd been told to forget, a woman she was told was better left in the past. But how could she forget her own mother? How could she just stop trying to find out what had happened to her? Why their lives had changed. She didn't even know how her own mother had died; Amélie just said she had died in the war, not of what or how. Every time she asked, Amélie's lips closed firm, like a clam. When pressed she'd say she didn't know, though Valerie knew, even then, that this wasn't true. All she really knew about her old life was that her grandfather had owned a bookshop in Paris, close to the river, and that somehow he was still alive, and perhaps he'd have the answers, the ones no one else would give her. It wasn't a fairy tale: it was a *quest*, into her history, into her past.

In the end, Freddy had bought the ticket.

CHAPTER FOUR

Paris

There was a single light on a string hanging over the piles of books scattered on the dusty floor, some still in their boxes, needing to be put on the shelves. Beneath these piles was the same herringbone pattern of wood as in the apartment upstairs, though covered in scratches. Vincent Dupont didn't see the dust, or the boxes. Or the overflowing shelves, not any more. If he had, he would have seen how much he needed the young woman who was unpacking her things upstairs.

As it was, he was deciding on whether or not the disruption was worth it. There was something about the girl's smile, a kind of innocence, that prodded at something he'd thought long buried away, deep inside – something he could well do without prodding right now.

He grunted, and got to work half-heartedly unpacking one of the big boxes on the floor, his lower back throbbing in protest. Vincent Dupont could locate one of the ten thousand novels he housed within the store in a matter of minutes. Or at least, that's how it used to be. Things were taking longer now. The dust was beginning to pile up, and sometimes a new order would come in and never be found again.

The bell tinkled, and he looked up with a frown. He let out a small, impatient sound and rolled his eyes, reaching for a cigarette as Madame Joubert walked in. She was a handsome woman, tall, broad of shoulder, who appeared larger than life with her bouncing red curls and glamorous waft of perfume. Dupont steeled himself for what she was about to say.

'And?' she asked, bouncing on her size forty-two feet, which, as usual, despite her considerable height, were clad in high heels.

'And what?' he grunted. 'Can I help you? Are you actually going to buy a book for once, Madame?'

Madame Joubert laughed as she tutted, 'Dupont, don't be a grouch. Is she here?'

'Who?' he asked. Though of course he knew perfectly well *who* Madame Joubert was referring to.

'Your new assistant. Where is she?'

He gave a shrug, stabbing in the direction of the stairs with his cigarette. 'A young English girl with an appalling sense of style is currently upstairs unpacking what should probably be thrown into the Seine. If that is who you mean.'

'Dupont, be kind. She said she was a student. And she's from England.' As if that excused it. Madame Joubert was the kind of person who pitied anyone who hadn't had the benefit of growing up in Paris.

It was Madame Joubert, who ran the popular flower shop next door, who'd suggested that it was time that M'sieur Dupont hire an assistant when she'd found him one day half unconscious on the shop floor, having fainted from low blood sugar. The doctor who'd been called to the scene had warned that M'sieur Dupont needed to quit smoking and get some help at the store – the trouble was, he'd said it in front of Madame Joubert, who was like a dog with a bone. In the end, Dupont had agreed to only one of those things. He'd quit smoking when he was dead. Madame Joubert had helped him place the advertisement for a bookshop assistant in *Le Monde*, and after he'd chased off several French applicants, and later, when (with much scathing laughter) he'd shown her the letter written by an English woman named Isabelle Henry, it was she who'd convinced him to take a chance. Someone who could knowingly rile a Frenchman like that was obviously, in Madame Joubert's opinion, made of stern stuff – and perhaps wouldn't be as easily frightened off as the others. An essential attribute, she thought.

Madame Joubert had read the English woman's letter, in perfect schoolgirl French, and decided that someone with a library degree seemed like a sign from the heavens. Ignoring Dupont's protests, she'd told him to write back and agree to her terms.

'I'd have to hear her voice, which would be painful enough.'

'Don't be ridiculous,' she'd said.

'She offered to cook,' he'd said, showing her the letter, stabbing at the girl's words with a gnarled finger. 'Of all the women in Paris who could look after me, you want an English woman to cook for me?'

Madame Joubert had scoffed. 'Because, Dupont, you dine at Michelin-starred restaurants every evening? Let's not pretend, my dear man, that you are some gourmand. When every day it's a baguette with the same *fromage et jambon* or a croissant for breakfast? I'm sure she can live up to those exacting standards.'

He grumbled, but, of course, Madame Joubert got her way in the end. He wrote to the English girl that evening, but he drew the line at her cooking for him.

Now, of course, he regretted giving in. She'd arrived, winsome and blonde, with enormous green eyes that looked as if they would tear up at the slightest bad word. How was he supposed to manage that? Besides, he couldn't look at her – she reminded him too much of his daughter Mireille, and that was enough to make him want to walk to the Seine and throw himself in, though he would never tell Madame Joubert that, of course.

It didn't take Valerie long to unpack. Two dresses, and another pair of black brogues. Some undergarments, two cardigans, three blouses, a corduroy skirt, a pair of slippers, three pairs of stockings and two night gowns – these were the total of her wardrobe at present, and they fitted easily into the first two drawers of the bureau with plenty of room to spare. She put the suitcase under the bed, then took a seat on the stool, moving the small kettle to the floor, and looked out at the courtyard. Beyond it she could just make out the top of the roof of the building next door. Even the rooftops in Paris told a story, she thought.

Then she squared her shoulders, splashed some cold water on her face, and went downstairs to find her grandfather.

She found, instead, the sizeable bulk of Madame Joubert.

Clotilde Joubert raised high arching eyebrows, and waved a hand with red painted nails. 'Ah, the English girl,' she said, opening her arms wide. 'Welcome.'

Valerie smiled as the woman introduced herself. 'I am Clotilde Joubert. I run the flower shop next door. I had heard that you were the new victim and thought I'd come and introduce myself – in case you ever need a reliable witness for the prosecution.'

There was a disgruntled sniff from M'sieur Dupont, who had taken his seat behind the desk in the corner again and was currently loading a piece of paper into a navy blue typewriter, a cigarette dangling from his lips.

'Ignore her, we all do.'

Madame Joubert shrugged a shoulder. Valerie got the scent of flowers, and wondered if it was her perfume or if it simply radiated from her pores. Either way it was inviting, and she liked the older woman immediately.

'I am Isabelle,' said Valerie. 'Isabelle Henry.'

'A French name?'

Valerie hesitated: should she tell the truth – that she was born in France? But before she could decide, Madame Joubert peered over her shoulder at the line that was forming outside her small shop. 'Excuse me. I must go back – I just wanted to come and say hello. Come in any time, when you need to have your faith restored that there is something good in this world…'

Valerie bit back a laugh.

There was another grunt from the back of the shop. 'That one spends too much time sniffing roses, it's rotted her brain.'

Valerie grinned. She could tell that despite their words, they were firm friends, or if not, at least as close to it as was possible.

M'sieur Dupont grunted at her to start emptying some boxes, and to use the stamp with a large G for Gribouiller on the inside cover. 'You don't use stickers?' Valerie asked.

The look he gave rivalled Medusa's. She took that as a no, and got to work. She feared, though it was nearing evening already, it was going to be a long day.

CHAPTER FIVE

Vincent Dupont was the kind of man who made first impressions count. He certainly lived up to the one he'd made on Valerie when she'd first arrived, and if it was possible, during her first week at the Gribouiller he grew even more cantankerous as the days went by.

It seemed the time for niceties had passed. Especially when it came to the smooth running of his bookshop – and any ideas she might have for its improvement.

He'd objected, his old blue-veined cheeks growing red, when she'd begun putting the books she'd started to unpack from some of the many unopened boxes onto the shelves, alphabetically. He shot up out of his chair fast, his blue eyes outraged.

'*Non, non!* I will explain the system to you: it is a well-oiled machine. *Attention.*'

Which was how Valerie discovered on her first day the first real hurdle of their relationship: the Dupont System. A system of organisation whereby books were ordered according to whether or not the author had lost his mind. This was followed by the year of publication, the only concession he made, as time could excuse some, but not all things. 'He didn't know better then,' he said, for instance, of Émile Zola (this mainly referred to the author's disdain for the Eiffel Tower, and not to his work, it later ensued), 'but Alexandre Dumas certainly should have,' throwing a copy of *The Three Musketeers* (his criticism, in the main, was based on its length and tendency towards over-romanticism) into the waste basket for emphasis. (A rather shocked Valerie promptly dusted it off and put it back on the shelf, when he wasn't looking.)

'Too flowery,' was the work of Molière, which went in a section labelled 'Migraines' in his almost illegible pencil scrawl on a small piece of paper tacked with a blue pin to the shelf, the word underlined several times by slashes of pencil.

'Too English,' was the only pronouncement for a slim volume of Wordsworth's poetry, which was put in a section called '*Anglais Fou*', crazy English. 'Yes, the countryside is a balm, *mon Dieu*, but pull yourself together, M'sieur Wordsworth, stiff upper lip and all that, *s'il vous plaît…*'

Dupont, it seemed, enjoyed nothing more than getting a rise out of his customers.

Valerie wasted her breath trying to explain that a system that didn't judge the reader's taste would perhaps result in better sales – surely the entire point of having a bookshop in the first place. This suggestion was met with two hands raised as if to scrub her words away, a snort of 'Pah', and a tirade about the fact that he'd had the shop for over forty years, and it was his duty – however tiresome the mantle of the burden – to stopper the rising swell of stupidity in the streets of Paris, which, he warned, grew with each passing day, by encouraging his loyal customers to avoid rotting their brains with drivel.

And yet his customers, few though they were, *were* loyal, Valerie couldn't help noting. Brave, too. They seemed to come more for the lecture from Dupont than anything else.

Like the man who left smiling, clutching his copy of Jane Austen's *Sense and Sensibility* proudly, even though he'd actually wanted to buy the latest James Bond book by Ian Fleming.

At dinnertime he made trout with roasted potatoes in what he called 'a fishwife butter sauce' that mainly consisted of butter and lemon, and that was, Valerie had to admit, delicious. 'My mother's recipe – she came from Marseille,' he explained, when she asked. 'Though she wasn't a good fishwife,' he said, with a chuckle that descended into a cough.

At first, he wouldn't elaborate on his mother, Margaux, except to say, 'She came to her senses, and came to Paris, leaving my father to his wine and his women in the South.'

Valerie didn't really know what to say to that, except to stop herself from exclaiming that her great-grandfather was a *philanderer*.

'But she had some money from her parents – that's how she bought this apartment.'

'How old were you when you moved here?'

'A boy. Six or seven. I opened the shop below at the age of fourteen.'

'Fourteen?'

He shrugged. 'It wasn't that unusual then, and we had the space.'

'Did you always want to run a bookshop?' she asked, imagining him as a small child reading books on the banks of the Seine, talking to students from the Sorbonne.

But he just snorted. 'Pah. What else was I going to do – open a bistro?'

Which was about as much opening up from him as she could expect.

Over the course of the week they fell into a routine. Monsieur Dupont arose at six and was in the shop by seven. Valerie made breakfast – he trusted her with the task of getting croissants from the bakery on the corner, at least. Though the coffee she made was drunk with curled lips, just as the baguettes she assembled were prodded at before he nibbled the edges, reluctantly. 'This *jambon*, where did you get it – the *supermarché*?' The supermarket was akin to the devil, she was to find.

'No, the butcher, the one you said.'

There was a sniff. 'He must be having an off day.'

A mere second later: 'The baguette…'

'What's wrong with it?' she sighed.

'It's stale,' he said, prodding the soft, chewy centre.

Valerie snorted. 'It came fresh out of the oven ten minutes ago. I stood in line for half an hour for that baguette.'

Another sniff. 'Maybe we should try the bakery on the Rue des Minuettes.'

Trying a bakery in another street was like stating he would travel to the moon. It was also an empty threat.

It became clear soon enough that no matter how much time passed, aside from the odd baguette, which he picked at, he point blank did not trust her in the kitchen, despite the fact that she insisted that she'd grown up with a French relative, which was how she'd explained her impeccable French.

'Pah, in England?'

'Have you even been to England?' she asked. 'I think you may be pleasantly surprised.'

This was met with a look of utter derision, as if she were a house cat trying to tell a lion how fierce she was.

'I grew up in London,' she explained. 'The food there is very good – perhaps not all restaurants, pubs and cafes are as fantastic as in Paris, yes, but there are definitely some that could give a few a run for their money.'

To her surprise, though, he nodded, waving a hand in a gesture of acknowledgement. 'Ah *oui*, London, that's different, yes. *Dickens*,' he said, with a small, concessionary nod. As if that one word and one man alone elevated the city in its entirety. There were to be no arguments against M'sieur Dickens, she was to find.

She frowned. 'But London is in England.'

He screwed up an eye, and waggled his hand as if to say it was and it wasn't. A pile of cigarette ash landed on the floor as a result. She wouldn't admit it to him, of course, but she supposed his opinion wasn't wrong.

His groaning certainly made the days go by fast.

His fuse was about the length of an eyelash, and it erupted regularly, and with vehemence. And then it was over just as fast, like a cloud passing over the sun, and she soon grew used to his outbursts.

Though the first few days, it had her clenching her fists, and her stomach roiling.

They had had their first real argument on the second day that she was there, when he'd attacked one of her favourite authors, calling Marcel Proust a waste of paper.

It had lasted precisely thirty-seven minutes, and he had paused only to make them coffee before continuing the argument. If she'd asked for tea that would only have made the argument last longer. He refused to stock it, saying it made the kitchen smell.

'You can't be serious?' she'd exclaimed, appalled about his opinion on Proust and not the tea (which was the reason for the kettle in her room, he had explained). 'The man's a genius. Some people think that he's had one of the greatest impacts on modern literature to date.'

'Pfft. Nothing more than a pretentious snob. Some good quotes, yes, but mostly self-indulgent waffle, when it takes three thousand pages to say what could have been said in three hundred. His editors should be shot.'

Valerie's mouth fell open. Proust was, well, *Proust.* It was like calling Shakespeare unlyrical, unpoetic, *a blip*. She narrowed her eyes. 'So it's the style of Hemingway, then, that you prefer. All short punchy sentences?'

He looked apoplectic. 'An American? Look, the day the French start taking lessons in style from the Americans is the day all of

France should decide, en masse, to go the way of the dodo, and with haste…'

Valerie's eyes popped. 'Well, unlike the dodo, the French are still here precisely because the Americans helped save Paris during the war.'

He sighed. 'I never said they weren't good soldiers. Or brave. But it is begging belief to say they know anything about style.'

'In literature or fashion?'

'Both.'

Valerie put her hands on her hips. 'Fitzgerald, Melville, Faulkner, for heaven's sake?'

'Pah.'

Then he looked at her and raised a finger, like a small white flag. 'Wait. Okay… I'll give you… Dickinson.'

'Dickinson?'

'Emily Dickinson. She made love to the dash. Made you want to use it more yourself. Now that *is* style. Actually, I have a volume somewhere – let's put it in the good section, eh? Celebrate the Americans who helped free Paris.' He was only being slightly mocking.

The good section was called simply '*Pas Mal*', not bad. These were the acceptable books one could buy. There weren't many.

The ceasefire lasted about ten minutes, when she discovered that Bram Stoker – inventor of Dracula – was a 'conspiracy theorist' and that Sir Arthur Conan Doyle was a fool, who played golf.

'What has that got to do with it?' she cried, exasperated.

He looked at her incredulously. 'Everything. No man can have poetry in his soul and play golf.'

This, Valerie privately thought, was a bit rich, considering no one in their right mind would ever accuse Dupont of having poetry in his soul. But she said anyway, 'He created Sherlock Holmes! He didn't need poetry.'

He looked at her. 'We all need a little poetry in our souls, or else, like Sherlock, we may as well snort cocaine up our nostrils to escape life.'

Monsieur Dupont's tirades certainly made the day go fast.

When she wasn't being subjected to his tirades, she spent her time walking along the streets of their arrondisement, stopping to watch the ducks on the Seine, and the march of schoolchildren from the École Élémentaire Levant on the corner of their street, where promptly at four p.m. they all trundled up to the baker's with their mothers and nannies for their *goûter* – a sweet tea-time snack to tide them over before dinner. So different from Valerie's youth, when four p.m. had often meant that she had a jacket potato to look forward to for her tea after a cold trudge in the snow.

There were boutiques, and cafes, and pavement stalls where people sold all manner of things, from art to jewellery and vinyl records, the street a village in itself.

At Le Bistro Étoilé next door, with its red and gold chairs that spilled over onto the cobbled pavements, she would watch as people sat in the hazy French sunshine of the afternoon, wrapped up in coats and scarves in the cold weather, sipping a *citron pressé* or a *café noir* while nibbling on a croissant – the only way a respectable Parisian had coffee, Monsieur Dupont had informed her, the first time he saw her adding milk to hers and had called her a peasant. She found that she rather liked the coffee black, just as she enjoyed exploring the streets of Paris on her afternoons off.

'I think he likes you,' said Madame Joubert, as Valerie's first week came to a close. 'I haven't seen him this happy in years.'

Valerie stared at the woman in shock. 'I think you are mistaken, Madame. I am fairly positive that he hates me.'

Madame Joubert laughed a throaty chuckle, tossing back her mane of red curls, as she added a deep pink calla lily to the flower arrangement she was working on. The shop was painted a rich, dark turquoise, and was bursting with blooms of all sizes, shapes and textures in galvanised steel buckets. Valerie was sitting across from Madame Joubert on a small wooden bench, sipping an aperitif that she had insisted on pouring for her when she'd strolled in with the start of a headache. Dupont's voice was still ringing in her ears, and she needed somewhere she could go to be away for ten minutes, before she attacked the old man with his own stapler.

'Don't be ridiculous. He looks like a young man again, *chérie*. There's a spring in his step. His eyes twinkle.'

Valerie snorted. 'That's allergies – and rheumatoid arthritis.'

Madame Joubert roared with laughter. 'That too – but still, it's good to see him so happy.'

When Valerie went back to the shop that evening, with a bulging bag from the fish market, she hoped that what Madame Joubert had said was true, and that he really was happy that she was there. She put the fish in the fridge, then tidied up the store, one of the few chores he actually allowed her to do – which was waging war on the years of accumulated dust – and thought about the week so far. They certainly had spoken a lot, but not about anything besides books, and food, and Paris. She hadn't been able to get him to speak about the war – even when she had brought up the Americans. When she'd asked about it he'd grunted and changed the subject. She hadn't pressed him too much, even though he had promised her in his letter that he would speak about what it was like running a bookshop during the Occupation. Perhaps he just needed more time.

A grunt had also been how he'd told her that he'd found her performance acceptable, and that he wasn't in fact going to be sending her home on the next train. 'I'm used to you getting the croissants in the morning now.'

Which was about as much praise as she could hope for, she supposed.

CHAPTER SIX

The cat was a mangy thing, just skin and bone and sinew, with bald patches in its once glossy black-and-white fur and a missing tail, which had been lost in a valiant fight with an orange alley cat some seven years before. The cat belonged, if it belonged anywhere, to the Gribouiller bookshop on Rue des Oiseaux, and to M'sieur Dupont, though he denied such a thing, *mais bien sûr*.

'Pah, that bag of old bones. What do I want him here for, eh, fleas?'

But still, there was fresh milk for the cat every morning, and when he thought Valerie wasn't looking, she caught him feeding it from his hand.

When he saw that she'd seen, he sniffed, saying that he didn't want to have the burden of carting the beast's body away if it died.

The bookshop cat didn't have an official name. If it did, it was *Le chat de M'sieur Dupont*, and later just Dupont, so sometimes you couldn't be sure if the neighbours were talking about the cat or the man. Valerie learned soon enough, though, that if it was with any degree of affection, it was almost certainly the cat.

The cat was circling now around a new delivery of books, which had been hastily dropped into the corner, rubbing his tail-less bottom on the edge of the box.

''E is so sweet,' said Madame Hever, one of Dupont's brave and fearless customers, who didn't mind that she was called a philistine for reading anything but Dickens, and began scratching the cat under its chin. He began at once to purr.

'*Non*, he is a pest,' said Dupont in denial, yet managing to acknowledge his virtue by adding, 'but at least he keeps the rats away.'

This was a lie, so Valerie knew, but she spared the cat (and the man) the shame of pointing it out, and got back to counting the stock.

She moved to take the empty box away, which was when she saw the hole in the wall. It looked almost like a bullet wound.

Her fingers touched the hole, making a small confetti of plaster rain down on the wooden floor.

'It does need a paint,' sniffed Dupont, shuffling over, 'but at least try not to make it worse.'

'It looks like a bullet hole,' said Valerie, straightening up with a frown.

He shrugged. 'That's because it is.'

Her eyes widened. 'What? How?'

He looked at her as though she were stupid. 'We are in the centre of Paris – there was a war, people used bullets.'

'In here?'

He shrugged again. '*Oui*.'

At her look of surprise, he sighed as he explained: 'That, *chérie*, was the work of a singular Nazi, who thought that the best way to deal with a book by Balzac was by putting a bullet through it. *Charmant*.'

It was Madame Joubert who provided more information about the bullet hole, when she brought in another box that had been delivered to the flower shop by mistake, and Valerie told her what Dupont had said.

Madame Joubert nodded, her mouth pursing in displeasure. 'Ah *oui*, I remember that day, how could I forget,' she said, her kohl-rimmed eyes unusually sombre, as Valerie came forward quickly to take the box from her. She put it in the corner of the shop next to the small red bistro set that she had turned into her own desk, complete with a spot for the cat and the telephone.

'It was that first week too – just after the fall of Paris – when they were really throwing their weight around, the Nazis. The one who did that,' she said, pointing at the wall, 'was a young man, with a small afterthought of a moustache, as if it was drawn in pencil. He couldn't have been out of shorts for long. I'd come into the shop to help Mireille – that was Dupont's daughter…' Her eyes grew sad, and she paused and touched her chest, just as Valerie's own heart began to thud at the mention of her mother's name.

'And in came these young men, dressed in brown, telling Dupont which books he now could and could not sell. Which went as well as you can imagine… When Dupont protested at the banning of one of the authors – I forget which –'

'Balzac, that's what Vincent said,' supplied Valerie.

'*Oui*,' said Madame Joubert. 'Balzac. Bang, he shot the cover. There's not much to argue against a boy and a gun.'

'Why didn't M'sieur Dupont close the shop?' asked Valerie.

'He was stubborn. Stubborn then. Stubborn now. Besides, I don't think there was anywhere he could go. His father was long gone, and his mother had died the year before. There was a cousin of some kind, but I believe she had already gone to England… I'm not sure.'

Valerie's heart started to pound as she realised that Madame Joubert must, of course, be referring to Amélie.

'So, they were stuck here in Paris, and Mireille wouldn't leave her father, even though he wanted to send her to the countryside which is where most of the people who could afford to fled. Though it wasn't that much better there, in the end.'

Valerie shook her head. 'It must have been terrifying seeing the Nazis descend on Paris like that.'

'It was. I will never forget it. We believed, like a lot of the French, that the Maginot Line would hold – then suddenly we were told by the government that we were fortunate, they had arranged an armistice – a ceasefire, though of course we all knew what that really was: *surrender*. We listened on the radio as they told us that now we must put down our weapons and stop fighting. There wasn't a soul alive in Paris who believed this was anything but *defeat*.'

Dupont walked in then, followed by the small mangy cat, the old man's face twisted in anger, even now. 'No, it was *betrayal*. They did nothing less than leave us like lambs for the wolves.'

Madame Joubert nodded. 'That too.'

CHAPTER SEVEN

'We watched as they marched into town, German soldiers marching past the Arc de Triomphe, with their tanks and cars – there were so many of them, an entire army of men in brown. I'll never forget that day…' said Madame Joubert.

Dupont looked down, his brow furrowed. 'Mireille's birthday,' he said softly.

The air grew tense, and Valerie held her breath; it was the first time he'd mentioned his daughter to her.

Madame Joubert's face was grave as she nodded. 'The fourteenth of June. She'd just turned nineteen. Not much younger than you are now, I suppose,' she said, looking at Valerie. 'You look a bit like her, you know?'

Valerie's heart stopped beating for a moment. Dupont frowned and spared her a glance; there was a small incline of his white head. He sighed. 'It wasn't the kind of present anyone could ever want – a city of Nazis.' His face was as dark as thunder. He shook his head, then turned and left the shop, his shoulders seemingly more stooped than ever.

Valerie made to go after him. But Madame Joubert placed a hand on her shoulder, stopping her. 'Leave him, *chérie,* it'll do no good to follow him. He's battling old ghosts now.'

Valerie went with Madame Joubert to the flower shop, where she made her a cup of tea, placing it before her on the wooden bench.

The shop was closed, and the early morning air sneaked in beneath the wooden doors and windows, stirring the exposed skin on Valerie's neck and face, making her shiver. She took a sip of the sweet tea and smiled. English Breakfast. Madame Joubert must have bought it especially. The older woman sat down across from her and resumed her work, showing Valerie how to trim a stem and place it into the waiting foam. Valerie breathed in the heady scent of the flowers, and began stripping the bottom leaves off a hothouse rose.

Between them the weight of Dupont's departure earlier was heavy with unanswered questions. 'It's still real for him, isn't it? Even now,' said Valerie, her gaze not taking in the colourful blooms of the shop, but looking outward, through the window and seemingly into the past. 'The war, I mean.'

She didn't have to say who she meant. Madame Joubert knew to whom she was referring. Her fingers shook slightly as she placed a lilac-hued hydrangea in the green foam, alongside a blush pink rose.

'Yes. For all of us, it's still real. That day when they came – it's hard to capture what we all felt – essentially we felt abandoned. Most people were fleeing in the streets, taking everything they could carry, going to friends or family in the countryside. Even our government had abandoned us – so it seemed when they moved to Vichy, leaving the city to the Germans… and the few French officials they approved of – the ones who had handed us over so easily. Overnight we were no longer citizens, but spectators, watching as the invaders took over everything. Imposing their rules, taking our homes, our food… rationing what had once belonged to us. Overnight, Dupont went from running a small business to being told by a bunch of snot-nosed boys how to live.'

As Madame Joubert spoke, she was swept back twenty years…

The boy who had shot the novel by Balzac came to the store frequently afterwards. Came to see the pretty blonde girl with the shocked blue eyes, and the full mouth.

Came to see how the nerve twitched in the old man's jaw, how his pale blue eyes blazed, and how hard it was for him not to take the boy by the scruff of his neck and throw him out of his shop. He enjoyed watching the old man's slow loss of power.

The boy wasn't the only Nazi soldier who came into the shop. There were many more over the course of the month following the fall of Paris.

When the last one had left for the day, Mireille closed the blind, even though it was only six o'clock and the sun was still shinning. She wanted to block out the day, turn the world dark to reflect her mood. She poured herself a glass of wine and took a sip. When the liquid spilled, she realised that she'd been shaking again without noticing.

Her father came and put a hand on her shoulder. It was knotted and tense, but she stilled at his touch. She looked up and saw that his face was worried, grave.

'It's not too late: you can go to the country still. My cousin, Amélie, she could help you.'

Mireille shook her head. 'I won't leave you, Papa.'

He gritted his teeth, took the cigarette he'd been keeping behind his ear, and put it between his teeth with a slight grunt. 'I don't want you to have to face this,' he said, pointing at the door, at the world outside, the world gone mad.

She looked at him, her blue eyes softening. 'No one wants to face this, Papa. No one. But we'll do it together, like everything else.'

She took another sip, then took a weary seat in the big armchair by the window, moving aside Tomas, the cat, and putting him on her lap. The wine was at last beginning to work.

'You know what most of these men… these Nazis buy from the shop?'

He frowned, flicked his ash into the ashtray on his desk. 'Let me guess: adventure stories. Something with bullets and bravado,' he said, pointing at the space in the wall where the half-grown blond idiot had shot the book.

She shook her head and scratched behind the cat's ears. He purred, lifting an orange tabby head to look at Dupont.

'Guidebooks to the city. It's like… to them they're on holiday.'

He blinked. He thought there wasn't much that could shock him now – not since the city was occupied – but that did.

'They're on holiday – and we're going through hell.'

'Yes.'

CHAPTER EIGHT

Valerie was tired. It felt as if the past few weeks had all hit her at once. The mattress in her small iron bed seemed to be made up of corkscrews instead of springs, each one finding ways to enact some revenge against her body, and no amount of turning made a difference. She couldn't remember the last time she'd had a full night's sleep.

On top of which, Dupont's snores echoed through the walls of the small apartment, and kept her awake most nights, along with her thoughts.

Bringing up the war had made Dupont's mood even more sour than usual.

He'd turned quiet, monosyllabic. A dark mood had taken over him, and didn't pass for most of the week. Despite the quiet this ensured, as well as the break from his outbursts, it made the days longer, and tenser somehow.

For the first time since she'd arrived she'd begun to really wonder at what she'd done – why she'd come. What would happen when she told him who she really was? What would he do? What if she came to love him…? Though there seemed little danger of that now, stranger things had been known to happen, she knew. What then? It had been easier to convince herself that his indifference didn't matter when he was a stranger. She'd seen how his face had turned when he spoke about the Nazis; it was a different kind of anger. It wasn't his usual disagreeable nature

– this was cold, hard, and she could tell it wasn't something he wanted prodded.

During the few hours of sleep that she snatched in the night, her dreams had been the same – the Nazis marching through the city, flags of spidery swastikas taking over everything, the removal of old street signs, replaced with ones in German highlighting their headquarters, the Paris streets in smaller letters beneath. She wondered when she woke up, her heart pounding, how her mind had filled in those images. Had she perhaps seen them in a newspaper somewhere? Though she couldn't quite remember where. At last, she greeted the dawn with bruise-like shadows beneath her eyes. She sat up, her mouth dry, her tongue parched, and reached for the glass of water on her bedside chair, and took a sip with a frown. The last dream had felt so real.

She was three years old, her blonde hair streaming out behind her, the red ribbon getting sucked up by the wind, and as she turned to chase after it, she heard Amélie's voice: '*Vite, vite, chérie*, there's no time.'

But it was her only ribbon. They weren't easy to get any more; Grand-père had said that she had to make this one last when he tied it to her hair each morning, tightly. She started to cry. Amélie hadn't tied it right when she'd done her hair, and now it was gone. Amélie ignored her crying, and told her to keep going. But Valerie was tired, not used to walking so far, and her feet had begun to throb in her thin shoes, the cold creeping into the toes. Amélie tugged at her arm again, not letting up.

'But I want to go home! This isn't the right way!' She didn't want to be with her any more, her 'aunt' whom she'd just met the day before – she was still a stranger, and now she was weary and sick of being polite. She just wanted to go home. 'Grand-père will be worried. Let's go back now,' she said, tugging Amélie's hand, and turning back towards the direction of the apartment.

It was getting late. This was the time they always played the game, the one with the cat and the string. Why was Amélie taking her so far away? Why was she going with this woman, who insisted that she call her 'Aunt' though she'd never met her before?

Her panic began to mount, and she began to sob. As they were going further and further away from the apartment, Valerie realised suddenly that they were on the wrong side of the river and it would take even longer to get home, yet still Amélie kept walking, dragging her along, finally picking her up despite her cries. 'No, I want Grand-père! Grand-père!'

'Enough, child,' said Amélie, cradling her to her chest as she ran, Valerie's head knocking into the woman's hard shoulder, her arms tight and unrelenting, even as she screamed…

Valerie woke up with a start, the sob still tight inside her throat, her heart feeling as if it may burst out of her chest. Was that just a dream? Or a memory?

The vision of herself as a child, playing some game with her grandfather, seemed real. More real than she would have thought.

And was it true – had her Aunt Amélie been a stranger? She rubbed her throat, struggling for breath, and went to the small sink, clutching it with both hands, her knuckles turning white. She splashed cold water onto her face and saw her reflection in the small vanity mirror; she looked grey. Was Amélie really a stranger when they met? Amélie had told her that she'd sneaked into the country especially to fetch her. Why?

She'd got the impression from the way Amélie had spoken that her grandfather hadn't been interested in raising his granddaughter, that he'd wanted her to be safe, yes, but that he didn't want to be her guardian. But that memory – or whatever it was – was something else, a long-ingrained habit of spending her days with the old man, of him looking after her, doing her hair in the morning, eating together, and playing with the cat long into the afternoon, just the two of them. That didn't seem like a man who hadn't been interested in his grandchild: quite the opposite. Why, then, would he give her up?

Valerie sat in the dark, and for the first time she felt the sorrow behind what had happened to her, felt the pain. For the first time, she admitted to herself that perhaps her being here, prising out these long-buried secrets, might just end up opening a wound she couldn't easily close.

If Valerie was somewhat reserved that morning, Dupont didn't notice. He was too busy fighting with his customers. She got stuck into the day's administration, cataloguing the stock in her neat handwriting on index cards, which she put into a wooden box on her small desk. Making a note of what had sold, and what new orders were needed.

When the large black telephone that Dupont had moved to her desk – he thought she responded better to the customers (this wasn't hard) – rang, she started, her heart thudding, so lost was she in her thoughts.

'*Bonjour*, Gribouiller,' she said in her polite assistant-librarian voice, a voice that couldn't seem to help whispering just a little around books.

'Ah *oui*, I am looking for something,' said a muffled voice on the line.

She frowned. 'Yes?'

'Something that I seem to have missed.'

Valerie frowned. 'Did you misplace something in the shop?'

Her eyes scanned the newly swept floor, noting the polished wood – her recent work from the day before – the neatly stacked books, the new window display along with her cut-outs of snow-flakes and frost to highlight the season… nothing looked amiss.

She glanced over at Dupont's desk, which of course looked like a tip, covered in overflowing ashtrays, paperwork, books and crumpled bits of paper, along with the cat.

'Yes, actually,' said the voice.

'Oh? Can you describe it, please, I'm sure I can put it aside for you if I find it.'

'That would be most kind, *merci.* Well, let's see, shall we? It's quite small for its age. Has long blonde hair, and wears these rather awful mustard-coloured skirts with brogues, but somehow manages to carry it off.'

Valerie frowned. 'What?'

'Look to your left,' said the voice.

She looked to her left.

'Your other left.'

Then she let out a squeal, and jumped up and down in her seat. Across the street, standing at a payphone, was *Freddy.* She could see his tall, lanky frame, his dark, tousled hair, and his wide grin from here. 'So, are you going to come and give us a hug or what?' he said, and she could hear the warmth in his voice.

'Yes!' she yelled. Then she jumped up and ran out of the shop, to M'sieur Dupont's, and indeed the cat's, utter surprise.

'Well?' asked Freddy, after she had at last let him go. 'Did you miss me?'

'Nah, hardly thought of you at all,' she said, giving his hair a sniff and closing her eyes in bliss. It still smelt the same, like peppermint and boy.

He put a thin arm around her. 'Me neither. Lunch?'

'Yes – let me quickly tell M'sieur Dupont.'

'Okay.'

'Okay.'

'You have to let me go first,' Freddy pointed out.

'Right,' she said, then grinned, reluctantly letting go of his string-bean arm and dashing back inside the shop.

She returned in seconds, and they walked to the bistro on the corner. From the flower shop window, she caught Madame Joubert's eye and her raised eyebrow. 'Very handsome,' she mouthed with her forever cherry-red lips, which made Valerie laugh.

'What?' said Freddy, who hadn't seen. His dark eyes crinkled at the corners, and she couldn't help staring at him too long, drinking him in.

'Nothing, never mind. Freddy, how are you here, why are you here? Tell me everything,' she said as soon as they'd sat down at a table on the cobblestone pavement and ordered coffees. Her big green eyes wide and shining, her cheeks rosy and lighting up the cafe, she seemed very alive. A group of chic Parisians looked up at her loud voice, then readjusted their sunglasses, taking sips from their short glasses of wine.

'Oh Val,' he laughed. 'Paris has rubbed off on you… you're all poise.'

She narrowed her eyes, but couldn't help her grin. 'Shut up and tell me why you're here.'

His eyes were alight with amusement as he took a cigarette out of his coat pocket, tapped it on the table twice, popped it between his lips and lit it, taking a deep drag. Then he handed it to her so she could do the same. He crossed his long legs, then unbuttoned his shirt collar. 'Well, to tell you the truth, the paper wanted someone to cover a political story here – so I volunteered to go.'

'Really?'

'Okay, I begged.'

'What?'

'Yeah, well, actually they'd already agreed to send Vile Jim.'

They both shared an eye roll. Jim Murphy was a slightly senior reporter who always seemed to get the best assignments, mostly because he was a bit of a bulldog. The trouble was that he liked to rub Freddy's nose in his victories. 'But I knew other papers would be interested – particularly if I could stay for a while – and Jim's a family man… so they agreed, mainly because now I can keep tabs on a few other leads. And I come rather cheap – basically I'll be a glorified private investigator. The job comes with a rat-infested apartment, a shared bathroom and practically no money, but I'm here, which is the main thing.'

She frowned. He had been getting pretty high up at *The Times*; this seemed almost a step back in some ways. 'Why would you agree to that?'

'Why do you think?'

'You were worried about me?'

'I was worried about you,' he agreed. 'And don't get soppy about this. But I missed you.'

She gave him a soppy look.

He laughed. 'I said, don't.'

'It's only been two weeks,' she said. Though she had missed him every second of that time.

'I don't think I've ever not seen your face for that long.'

Valerie laughed. 'Except for that time you went to Spain to be like Hemingway for a month? Or you decided to try living in a van down in Devon for a fortnight writing your novel, before you realised you quite liked showers.'

'Okay, yes, besides those. Honestly now – and don't lose it with me – but I just want to be here, however this goes. If it ends up going wrong – this thing you're doing with your family, pretending to be someone else – then I need to know you aren't here falling apart all by yourself, with nowhere to go. If it goes well, then, you know, I want to know that too.'

She took his hand and squeezed it. 'Thanks, Freddy. Did you have to break it to all the other girls?'

He shrugged. 'Yeah, that's why it took two weeks: lots of paperwork.' He grinned.

When she got home, she found Madame Joubert and Dupont sitting in the living room in the apartment upstairs, having a glass of wine.

'Well, well, wonders never cease,' said Madame Joubert, her full cherry lips splitting into a wide grin. 'Our little Isabelle… I would not have expected to see you run off like that into the arms of a man.' Her eyes scanned Valerie's brogues, her long corduroy mustard-coloured skirt. 'You never can tell with a librarian,' she said in a stage whisper, which made Dupont choke on his wine, as she chuckled.

Valerie made things worse by blushing.

'It was only Freddy.'

'Oh, Freddy,' said Madame Joubert, her kohl-rimmed eyes sparkling. 'I like him already. Tell us about this Freddy.'

So she did.

'He's a journalist. My oldest friend – that's all he is really.'

Even Dupont scoffed at that. Which was when she admitted the truth to them: that she'd been in love with him since she was a girl, and then the even more heart-breaking truth, which was that to Freddy she would always be that little girl. 'He's had dozens of girlfriends. I suppose I was always waiting for him to one day magically see me as something besides the girl next door, something besides a sister. That's why he's here – he's on assignment, but he's just checking up on me, being a good "big brother".'

Valerie felt her mood deflate as she admitted the truth to herself. There had been a moment when she'd almost convinced herself that Freddy's feelings for her had changed, had turned romantic, but she could see now that she was probably fooling herself, once again.

Madame Joubert burst out laughing. 'Ah, Dupont, do you remember being so young and so foolish?'

Dupont looked shocked. 'Me? Pah, never.'

Madame Joubert nodded, eyeing his white, slightly balding head, his stooped shoulders, and sighed. 'I suppose you were born old…'

He made a grunting noise and she continued.

'My darling Isabelle, a boy does not run to Paris to check up on his sister.'

'Course he does. He was worried about me.'

Madame Joubert shook her head.

Dupont shook his head too. Valerie was glad to see that the dark mood that had grabbed hold of him this past week had shifted somewhat, and he was back to being his usual cantankerous self.

Madame Joubert nodded. 'I had two brothers myself. I can't say they ever worried that much about me, not to the extent that they would follow me to another city. *Non, chérie*, I'd say that that's the work of a boy in love.'

Valerie swallowed, trying to stem the sudden surge of hope her words had caused. 'Stop it, please, Madame,' she said, taking a sip of her wine. 'I might believe you, and then I'd really be in trouble.'

Madame Joubert's large dark eyes were surprised. 'Why would that be trouble?'

'Because it's probably not true.'

'Maybe, though I doubt it – don't you think it's time you found out?'

She swallowed. Maybe. Though the idea of having things become strained between them filled her with dread. How could you tell your oldest friend that you were in love with him and not have that change everything?

While Dupont snored on the sofa, Madame Joubert poured them some more wine, getting up to put another log on the fire. It was cosy in the apartment, the windows offering a view that stretched in the distance to the lights of Paris, with the Eiffel Tower far beyond.

Valerie took a sip of wine, and looked at Madame Joubert, and shook her head.

'What?'

'Well, it's just you're so nice. I mean, Dupont is…'

'Dupont,' said Madame Joubert. 'Yes.'

'But you are friends.'

Madame Joubert smiled. 'Yes. We are. The truth is,' she said, waving a hand when Valerie shot a glance at Dupont. 'Oh, don't worry, *chérie*, he could sleep through Armageddon… Well, as I was saying, the truth is we are the only ones left, we're family now. I used to be friends with his daughter,' she explained.

Valerie paused mid-sip. 'Mireille?' she asked.

Madame Joubert's eyes grew sad as she nodded.

Valerie looked from Dupont to Madame Joubert, and whispered, trying her best not to seem too eager, 'What was she like? Was she like him?'

'Mireille?'

Valerie nodded, and Madame leant her considerable bulk back against the sofa, her magenta curls brushing against the soft linen, and sighed. 'She was' – she raised her eyes to the ceiling, as if to ward off the sudden onset of tears – 'wonderful, truly. We were best friends from the time we could walk and talk. Neighbours – like you and your Freddy,' she said with a soft smile. 'Mireille's mother, Jeanette, had died when she was young, so Dupont raised her all by himself. They were a pair, the two of them. Arguing all day, like an old married couple, and always about books.' She laughed. 'A little like the two of you, now,' she said, then chuckled.

'I think it's one of his biggest regrets really – that he didn't insist that she go with the others: the ones who were fleeing Paris for the countryside in their droves when the Nazis arrived, when she had the chance. But I knew Mireille and there was no way he would have persuaded her to go – not without him. What happened wasn't his fault.'

'What do you mean?'

They were whispering, careful not to wake the old man.

'I mean, how things turned out. He couldn't have known. None of us knew what would happen – we'd hoped they'd be here a few months and then be gone, driven back by the allies… we couldn't know what was to follow. In a way that was a blessing, and a curse.'

CHAPTER NINE

1940

Clotilde slunk into the bookshop, her face dark as thunder, her mouth uncharacteristically un-lipsticked and sagging at the corners. Her hair was flat, devoid of its usual curls and bounce. She looked like a large balloon that had developed a slow puncture, and she was, if possible, shorter somehow, as if she had been cut down at the knees.

Mireille looked up from the Nazi officer, a young man with a crew cut, ice blue eyes and sharp, white teeth, who was trying his best to charm her, while asking her about the best place to have duck à l'orange, and whether she would like to accompany him sometime. Mireille frowned, her mouth making a small 'o' of surprise as she stared at her friend, her eye falling at last on the badge like a yellow beacon on her friend's jacket. She watched as Clotilde sloped into the corner, half hidden behind a small stand of paperbacks, waiting for her.

Mireille's hands shook and she swallowed, giving the soldier a thin, tight smile.

'Is that the time?' she exclaimed, glancing at the clock on the wall in the far corner, though she didn't read it. 'I'm afraid, sir, I have to close the shop,' she told the officer suddenly, standing up. 'I have a dentist appointment, which I nearly forgot. I'm already late, if you don't mind…'

The officer left with a laugh, telling her to look after her pretty smile, suggesting that he'd call on her again some time soon for dinner if she was free. Mireille's face hurt from gritting her teeth in a pained grimace of a smile. As soon as he was gone, she locked the door and put up the 'closed' sign, even though it was barely past ten in the morning.

She turned to her friend, her blue eyes wide and filled with fear. 'So, it's true.' She came over to touch the large yellow star tacked onto the jacket. 'You have to wear this now?'

Clotilde nodded. Her eyes were scared too, which was what shocked Mireille most – her friend, larger than life, bolder than anyone she knew, was never afraid of anything.

'Can't you just take it off?'

'No, they said it's the law now and if any Jew doesn't wear it then we could get sent to jail – there's a list with all our names…' she explained.

Mireille had heard the rumours, of course she had, but despite all that she'd seen and heard so far – including the crazy man who'd shot a book in their shop – she hadn't dared to believe that the Nazis would be asking the city's Jews to identify themselves.

'Why are they doing this?'

'Why? It's because of him, Hitler, their fearless lunatic of a leader – he hates us.'

'I know… but—'

'There needs to be a reason beyond the fact that we are different?'

'How? How are you different? Do you not bleed?' she said, quoting Shylock in *The Merchant of Venice*. It was gallows humour, but Clotilde appreciated it all the same.

'Not enough, clearly,' said Clotilde with a wry twist to her lips.

Mireille kissed her friend's cheek and embraced her. 'Stay here tonight, with us.'

Clotilde nodded. She didn't want to be in the apartment next door, alone. Her brothers were fighting in the war, and her mother was in the countryside, with her sisters. Only Clotilde had stayed behind. She'd declared that she would join the resistance – though as the days passed she wasn't sure if there even was such a thing as yet. But she vowed she would be ready for it when it arrived.

'I'll make us some tea, and we can pretend, just for a moment, that the world hasn't gone completely mad,' said Mireille.

'I think for that you'd better open up a bottle of wine instead.'

Mireille nodded. 'Yes.'

But the world had gone mad. Well and truly mad. And as far as Mireille was concerned, that madness took the form, for the most part, of the young Nazi soldier named Valter Kroeling who'd made it his mission, ever since that first day he'd come inside the shop firing his pistol at the book, to spend as much time as he could in the bookshop. A month later he had declared himself the new manager of the store, to her father's complete outrage.

Mireille had had to warn her father to keep his temper. Already the Nazis were making short work of the men in the city; you could be sent to a labour camp or jail just from opening your mouth. She didn't want that for her father.

Valter Kroeling came into the shop, shortly after Clotilde had come around with the news that Jews now had to identify themselves, to declare that from now on half of the bookstore would need to make room for a division of Official Correspondence. This consisted mainly of a small press that would soon form part of the German propaganda wheel. They would also be using the bookshop to store pamphlets and newsletters to encourage the people of Paris to obey their new rulers.

A few days later, seeing Clotilde step inside the shop one afternoon, Valter Kroeling marched to Mireille's side to tell her that her Jewish friend was no longer permitted to walk through the front door, and should enter only through the service entrance around the back from now on. 'Like the rest of the riff-raff. But who knows,' he whispered into her ear, moving aside her long, silken hair, causing the tiny hairs on the back of her neck to stand on end in revulsion. 'For a kiss, maybe I can look the other way.'

She pulled away, forcing out a tight smile. She wanted to retort that he wasn't a man at all, just a boy playing dress-up, but she clenched her jaw and gritted out through her teeth: 'I'll see my friend at the back as you advise. M'sieur,' she added, like a hiss.

His face hardened. 'If that is what you wish.'

'It is.'

He looked at her, and cocked his head to the side. Mireille could see along his forehead a string of pimples. His pink, fleshy hand strayed to the top of her linen blouse, touching the collar, and leaving behind a small mark from his ink-stained fingers. 'There is still time to change your mind. I can wait for you to come around, if you know what I mean.'

She had to stop herself from batting his hand away.

Behind her someone cleared his throat.

It was another Nazi, one she hadn't seen before. He was a big man with dark blond hair and vivid green eyes.

'Mademoiselle,' he said. 'My apologies, I was wondering if you could help me.' He saluted Valter Kroeling, who stood reluctantly back from Mireille. Kroeling greeted the man with, '*Heil* Hitler. Herr Stabsarzt Fredericks.'

The doctor nodded his greeting and turned to Mireille. 'I was hoping that you had a French to German medical dictionary? I'm afraid that I am slightly rusty on my French medical terminology.'

Mireille was for once genuinely grateful to see another soldier, and went to check their catalogue in haste – anything to get away from Valter Kroeling and his grasping hands. 'I am not sure if we stock anything like that, M'sieur, but I will check. If not I can order one for you from the publisher.'

'That would be most kind,' he said, sounding surprised.

A muscle twitched in Mireille's cheek.

'It's what I would do for any customer.'

He frowned. 'Yes, I see.'

Mireille looked away. She had seen how some women were treated by the French for being too kind to the Nazis. There wasn't exactly a guidebook on how they were meant to behave. How should you act towards what were for all intents and purposes your captors? All she – along with the other women she knew – wanted to do was to tell them all to go to hell. The trouble was what happened when one did. They had all seen and heard officers lose their poise, striking an older woman who spat in a Nazi's face, carting them off to labour camps or worse… the things they did to some of them behind closed doors. What balance did you strike – how friendly was friendly enough to let them leave you alone?

'I'm afraid we don't have a medical dictionary – but I can order you one, as I suggested.'

'Thank you,' said the officer.

She nodded, and took down his name and telephone number for when the book was in stock.

He hesitated, then asked, 'They are setting up a printing press in here?' He gestured at the officers who had taken over half of the shop and commandeered the stock room.

She bowed her head, her smile thin, her eyes dark. 'We are allowed to keep this half of the store,' she said between clenched teeth. 'We are grateful.'

He nodded, and said again, 'I see.'

The pity in his eyes was too much and she looked away, then started when he leant his face near hers, and whispered, 'Be careful of Herr Kroeling.'

'M'sieur?' she asked, stepping back.

He straightened and his face was impassive. 'Remember what I said.'

She watched him go, then frowned. How bad was Valter Kroeling if his own people felt the need to warn her about him?

CHAPTER TEN

1962

The Cafe De Bonne Chance was filled with the sound of soft jazz. Through the fog of smoke and laughter, Valerie found Freddy sitting in the back facing the window, his battered green portable typewriter on the table, his long limbs crossed, a pencil clutched between his teeth. His messy dark hair was ruffled from where he was twisting it between two fingers, a habit he had had since he was child, whenever he was thinking about something. Valerie had often wondered if one day there would be a bald spot where his fingers played, but so far, so lucky.

He looked up and flashed her a grin, revealing the even teeth in his tanned, ruddy face, and his dancing brown eyes.

He'd been scribbling away in a notebook, which he closed when he saw her.

She ordered a *citron pressé* and marvelled at the sight of Freddy Lea-Sparrow in Paris.

When she sat down he gave her a heart-stopping wink.

She caught her breath. Could she actually do as Madame Joubert had advised and ask him straight out if he'd come here because he was in love with her? She gave a nervous laugh.

At his puzzled look, she chickened out and asked, 'How's your flat?'

'Well, I think it might classify as a garret, actually, lucky me. I mean, I couldn't have come to Paris as a writer and live in anything but a garret, you see – there's a certain expectation, a standard one must keep.'

She grinned and took a sip of the lemon juice the waiter brought over. 'What classifies a flat as a garret, exactly – is it because it's in the attic?' she asked with a frown.

'Yes, but see, that could easily be a penthouse, if it's not careful. There's no danger of that in my garret, though. First there's the fact that I can touch both walls by standing in the middle—'

'Ooh, me too, in my room.'

He laughed. 'So we're a pair. Still, I have a broken sink, the smell of mould, and a distant view of the brothel on the corner. Not too shabby either – they use red velvet for decor. And it's in Montmartre, so apparently all is forgiven.'

'Really?'

'Yes, except that it's not that bad, and the brothel is really just one lone prostitute by the name of Madame Flausier, who bakes the best apricot *tarte tatin* ever, and is not shy about making friends with strangers.'

Valerie's mouth fell open, shocked. 'Fred-dy.'

He grinned. 'She's seventy-three. I suppose if I were interested, she might take herself out of retirement…'

She laughed and poked him in the ribs. 'Stop teasing.'

'Impossible.'

She squeezed his arm. That *would* be impossible.

'So?' he said, giving her his interrogation look.

'What?'

'The bookshop – your grandfather? How's it all going? I had to move to bloody Paris just to get an update. You know that there are these things called telephones now, readily available, right? As well as letters? You could have tried one?'

She nodded. 'I know, sorry. I just had to be careful – what if I wrote to you and you wrote back calling me Valerie… or if Monsieur Dupont read the letter…'

'Val, I'm a journalist – I'm not an idiot.'

She shrugged. 'Yeah.'

'So what's he like?'

She told him.

They had lunch and moved on to wine, and by the end of her break, when she needed to get back to the bookshop, they had barely scratched the surface.

Freddy's eyes were serious. 'I'd like to meet him.'

'I'd like that too, but you're going to have to remember not to call me Valerie – promise me, Freddy. If you say it even once, I think he'd know. He's already said that I remind him of his daughter.'

Freddy was surprised. 'But then surely you should just tell him?'

She shook her head, bit her lip. 'Not yet. They're sort of opening up to me now, I just—'

'They?'

'Monsieur Dupont and his neighbour – Madame Joubert, mainly,' she had to admit, 'started telling me about my mother, about the Occupation – I think they need someone to talk to about it, though of course, Monsieur Dupont seems to clam up at any mention of the war. He just shuts down, seething with this unspent anger. I don't know how he'd take it if I told him.'

'What do you mean?'

'Monsieur Dupont is a bit of a wild card – Aunt Amélie called him mercurial, which is true, but he's – I don't know – easily riled, and he would be furious, possibly, thinking I'd tricked him. I just want to know more before I say anything. I feel that it's bigger than just telling him who I am – it's this chance I hadn't factored in when I got here. To hear about my mother – to find out who she was before she died, to find out *how* she died, even. And if I tell them who I am, I might risk having them stop, and I just don't want to risk that. Not yet, not after I've finally found a small part of her again.'

Freddy gave her hand a squeeze. He didn't need to say more; it was that simple gesture that said, I understand. I get it. She wished she had the courage at least to tell Freddy how she felt about him, and have one thing in her life out in the open at the moment. But when a pretty waitress walked past and he gave her a smile, Valerie stopped herself again. Right then the weight of all the things she needed to say felt like a lead ball sinking inside her chest, making even breathing difficult.

CHAPTER ELEVEN

The apartment was quiet, the dawn sky the colour of an old bruise, pewter grey and silent. Not even the birds had begun their song as Valerie slipped out of her bed, and got the old battered suitcase from underneath, placing it on top. In the inside pocket was the photograph Aunt Amélie had given her when she was a little girl. It was the only photograph she had of her mother. It was black and white, and showed a young Mireille, with long blonde hair, sitting by a window, her legs tucked beneath her. There was a cat in her lap, and she was laughing as she looked down at it.

Valerie touched the photograph now, and whispered, 'What happened to you? Why wouldn't anyone tell me?'

It hardly seemed real that she was here in this apartment, where her mother had grown up – where she as a child had spent her first early years; she was more sure of that now than ever. Sure even that once, a long time ago, this had been her room. That she had wanted the room painted blue, like her mother's eyes.

But was that true, or just a product of her imagination? How much of what she thought she remembered was just a desperate mind trying to fill in the missing parts of her own history? She put the photograph back inside the suitcase and pushed it beneath the bed.

If nothing else, she reminded herself – no matter how painful it could be, how much this could all go wrong – at least she would know who she was in the end, who she'd once belonged to. Her mother deserved that – the woman in the photograph with the kind face, and apples in her cheeks, deserved for her daughter to know who she was.

Valerie had become like a magpie, collecting everything that she saw or heard about her mother, which she assembled, like different sized twigs scattered with jewels and junk, to piece together a nest-like shell of who Mireille had been. She found samples of her handwriting on old index cards and in the margins of books, a cushion that she had made with the word *Gribouiller* stitched in thread, a watercolour painting of spring flowers in bloom hanging on the wall, with a faint signature at the bottom, a cursive M in the corner. She had been here. Had walked across these floors, slept between these walls. She had laughed and cried here, and somewhere, hidden from sight, was more of her story, if only Valerie could find the right key, the right words to prise the memories from Dupont and Madame Joubert's lips.

So she looked for things, ways to remind them, to tempt them, as painful as it was, to share their stories, and take her back with them into the past, so that her mother might live somehow, now, and in the future with her.

It was harder with Dupont, of course. He didn't open up easily, especially about the past. But when he did, it was as welcome as gentle rain on hot baked earth.

It was the simple admissions that sometimes fell from his lips that stopped her heart.

Like the day she picked up a copy of *The Secret Garden* that had been left behind on a table, and lingered over the pages, reading the first words, and he came past and touched her shoulder, his voice a little sad as he paused. 'That was Mireille's favourite when she was a little girl. She must have read it a thousand times – she used to carry it with her everywhere. Whenever we went somewhere and I said, "Go and get a book for the road," she'd dart inside in a flash to get that one, even though we had all of this to choose from,' he said, his hands taking in the wealth of books in the shop.

He smiled at the memory, though his eyes looked sad.

Valerie looked up at him, her heart beating faster.

'She always used to say that when—' He stopped then cleared his throat, his shaking hands reaching for his cigarettes, a frown between his eyes.

'She used to say…?' prompted Valerie.

He sighed, his gaze falling on the table for a moment, the pile of paperbacks that needed to be returned to the shelves. 'She used to say that she couldn't wait to share it with her children. Maybe start a garden of her own one day with them, if she had any.'

Valerie's throat constricted when she realised that somehow, Mireille had found a way to share her favourite story with her child after all. 'It's my favourite book too,' she breathed.

Tears pricked her eyes as she remembered. There had always been an old, yellow-papered, dog-eared copy in her room in London, always. It was kept on her nightstand since she could remember. It had its own smell, the pages buckled from when she'd taken it with her into the bath, and it had slipped and she'd had to dry it out in the sun. Or the time she'd got strawberry jam on the corners, when she'd stayed home from school with the mumps and it was the only thing that really made her feel better. It was that sort of book, the kind that always came off the shelf, which was more precious because of its wear and tear, and its Velveteen Rabbit type of love.

Valerie couldn't remember now where the book had come from – was it from her mother? Had it been taken with them on the day that Amélie and she had fled the streets of Paris when she was a little girl? How had she not known that all this time?

He smiled, touched her shoulder again, just an awkward pat really. 'She would have liked you, I think,' he said, before he shuffled away, leaving Valerie rooted to the spot, trying not to cry.

Freddy always said that if you looked hard enough for a story, you found one. Every time Dupont was out of the apartment, she looked. Looked for letters, for photographs, for anything that would tell her about what had happened to her mother, about who she was.

As the dawn coloured the sky a soft damson, she got dressed and went downstairs to start the day, measuring out several heaped spoons of the rich black coffee for the cafetière. She fetched two mugs from the cabinet, ready in wait.

She could hear him beginning to stir upstairs – the way one knee cracked when it straightened and the loud popping of old joints had become familiar sounds, greeting the start and the end of each day like bookends.

The cat was at the door, and she opened it to let him in. He took his position on top of Dupont's desk, settling in for the day.

She allowed herself a grin when, not long after, Dupont came down, greeting her with a nod, then took up his own position at the helm in the stuffed armchair.

It was a Saturday, which was always a busy day in the shop. Word had got out that there was a new bookseller at the Gribouiller in the few weeks that Valerie had been working there, and some of the customers who had vowed never to return, with shaking fists at Dupont, had begun to slink back in. Perhaps they sensed that she was less likely to offer a running commentary on their purchases, such as he was doing right now, to one poor soul who had come in to buy a copy of *Wuthering Heights* by Emily Brontë. She was a young woman with a long curtain of hair, parted precisely in the middle, and she was turning pink at Dupont's words. '*Mon Dieu*, save me from the moors and Heathcliff,' he lamented, shaking his head and putting the book aside on the table. 'Why not try *Jane Eyre* rather? If you insist on reading the Brontës. Or *The Tenant of Wildfell Hall*... very under-appreciated, that – and quite as good really.'

The girl's blushes were increasing and Valerie came past to save the day, picking up the book and taking the girl by her wrist to her own desk to complete the sale, throwing a comment over her shoulder at Dupont: 'Monsieur, Heathcliff will not be denied – you can prescribe vegetables all you want, but the heart won't be fooled by potatoes for chocolate.' She winked at the girl, who left the shop clutching her book to her chest.

'Pah,' was all Dupont said. Later, though, she could have sworn she heard him laughing.

Later that day, when he left the store to take the weekly earnings to the bank, her eye fell on his desk, and she bit her lip. He became like a bear with a thorn in its paw if she even dared to empty the ashtrays on it. It was covered in books, crumpled bits of paper and memories. He locked one of the drawers every evening, putting the little brass key into the pocket of his cardigan. It was possible that some of the answers she was looking for were hidden there.

The trouble was, if she was caught looking in that desk, it could bring everything to an end sooner than she would like. And she didn't want that, not now. Still, she knew that he would be gone for at least an hour: it was the perfect opportunity.

As soon as she saw that he was safely down the street, with his distinctive shuffle and a cigarette clutched between his teeth, she raced to the desk, steering clear of the cat's accusing eyes as he watched her carefully rifle through the scattered papers and paperbacks littering the surface. There was nothing there. She tried the drawer, which was locked. But then she spotted his cardigan hanging on the hook by the door, and found that she was in luck – the key was inside, meaning he hadn't yet opened the drawer since the night before. She went back to the desk and opened it, surprised to find that the drawer was much neater than she would have thought, though completely full of papers and letters. Her heart started to beat fast when she saw that there were dozens of photographs, too. She picked up a few and took a seat in the armchair, holding up one that made her catch her breath. It was of her mother, and it was in *colour*, slightly faded by time, but still remarkably preserved. It was the first time she had seen the colour of her mother's hair, a silvery pale blonde, and her eyes, which were darker than Dupont's, almost navy, but startlingly blue in her heart-shaped face. The eyes looked sad somehow, though she was smiling. Her face was so similar to Valerie's.

She touched it with a frown, tears smarting her eyes.

'What are you doing?' said a voice behind her, and Valerie dropped the stack of photographs and letters in fright.

She looked up to find Madame Joubert staring at her, hands on her hips, imposing in the pale afternoon light. Valerie swallowed, and quickly bent to pick up the letters and photographs, shoving them quickly back into the drawer. Her hands shook as she faced the older woman.

'I…' She hesitated; how much had Madame Joubert seen? There was no way she could pretend that she hadn't been snooping. The evidence was obvious. What would happen if she told Dupont?

She bit her lip, and attempted a lie, which sounded flat even to her own ears. 'I wanted to tackle his desk, clean it up while he was gone – it's such a mess.'

At Madame Joubert's darkening frown she could see that she wasn't going to fall for that – she had seen her with the photographs and the letters. Valerie swallowed. 'And h-his drawer was open,' she lied. 'And I got curious, I'm sorry. I was curious about him and Mireille – and what happened during the war,' she said truthfully.

To her surprise, Madame Joubert's face softened, and she came forward. The photograph Valerie had been looking at earlier had fallen behind the chair and Madame Joubert bent to pick it up. When she straightened, she put a hand on her heart. She stared at it, blowing out her cheeks, making an 'o' of her red lips, her eyes pooling with sudden tears. 'I'd forgotten about this – back then it was quite something to have a colour photograph, you know, during the war.'

Valerie blinked. 'This was taken during the war?'

Madame Joubert nodded. '*They* took it,' she said, and her lips grew thin, pursed, as she curled them in distaste. 'The Nazi officer who shot the hole in that wall – they wanted it for their *magazine*.' She said the last with disdain.

Valerie frowned, and Madame Joubert's face turned dark, pinched. 'Only the Nazis could afford to print things in colour then.'

CHAPTER TWELVE

1940

Mireille waited for Clotilde at the back door, hating that this was what they had been reduced to. She was tired, with dark shadows beneath her eyes. Since the Germans had taken over most of the shop, all she heard was their deep, staccato voices in her ears all day, each word like a hammer on her nerves, and she couldn't bear it any longer; she longed for peace. Peace also from the tightly wound spring that was her father, who looked as if he were ready to snap at any moment and throttle Valter Kroeling with his bare hands. Throttle him for having those dangerous, watery blue eyes that trailed his daughter everywhere she went, like a bad scent.

'Can I help you with something, old man?' Kroeling had asked the previous afternoon, noting how Dupont's face turned red as he watched him stare at his daughter, as though she were prey.

'Yes, you can help me greatly by going to he—'

'Papa!' interjected Mireille, her voice shrill with the warning, and her father stopped, reluctantly, his lips making a loose 'pfff' sound, like a tyre with a slow puncture. Mireille's jaw clenched as Kroeling's eyes glinted in triumph. The last time he'd spoken against Kroeling the Nazi had threatened to shoot her father, and she'd had to watch as he struck him with surprising force, knocking him off his feet. Seeing her father lying on the ground, a small trickle of blood leaving his lips, glaring up at the Nazi, Mireille had had to run to him and beg him not to say another word. Since then, he had had to keep his temper. His life depended on it.

As it was, Mireille could deal with Kroeling's stares, the way his eyes followed her everywhere, the way she had to wait until his back was turned before she went to the toilet in case he followed her in, but she couldn't bear the thought of something happening to her father as a result.

Mireille leant against the door now. She was nineteen years old, but at that moment she felt closer to forty. She prayed, even though she had long since stopped beseeching the heavens for help, for something to befall Valter Kroeling – a bullet, a knife, or at the very least for him to be taken somewhere else – but he was always there whenever she turned, with his moustachioed smile, and his sharp pointed teeth ready to draw her blood, like a parasite sucking the life right out of her.

Which was why, when Clotilde came up the street, her stride strong, her shoulders straight despite the star she was now forced to pin on her clothing while the other women her age wore whatever they liked, her eyes fierce, Mireille knew something had changed. Something, she hoped, for the better.

'Not here,' said Clotilde under her breath. 'Let's go to the park.'

She nodded. They walked quickly along the Seine till they entered the park. The weather had grown cool; there was the scent of rain and something else in the air, like possibility.

When she looked at Clotilde, she saw that for the first time in weeks her red hair seemed to shine and bounce again, and that she had her customary lipstick on. As they walked further into the park, the sound of leaves crunching beneath their feet, she found out why.

'I've joined the resistance,' she whispered, linking her arm through Mireille's.

Mireille's blue eyes widened. 'Clotilde!'

'Shhh.'

'Clotilde, really?' She was breathless, partly with nerves, partly with excitement. For the first time in days she felt something inside her shift, like a crack of light in a darkened room.

'Yes. There are a few of us. We are painting signs, messages.' Her lipsticked mouth twitched with something close to amusement.

'Signs and messages? Of what?'

'That Paris will never be theirs. That we are here – and we are growing stronger every day.'

'But what does that do – how does that help?' asked Mireille.

'It helps to show the people of Paris that they are not alone. It shows the Germans that they haven't conquered us all, not yet.'

They had been walking for some time when Clotilde pointed to a huge graffitied wall, dripping with black, oozing paint. It said, 'Resist.'

Mireille turned to her friend, her eyes shining.

By the time they'd left the park, she had already decided to join.

The trouble was, later that night, she thought of what joining would really mean. To her. To them. To her father most of all. Was it worth risking her life for a few graffitied signs? Especially if that meant that she left her papa alone with the Nazis? Alone with Valter Kroeling? She shuddered at the thought. How long before he got himself killed if she were gone? As it was, he was barely hanging on by a thread. It had become apparent that the safest way to keep him from going to jail was for him to spend as much time away from the bookshop as possible, and even that was like trying to stop the tide. There was nothing they could do. Even if they wanted to close the shop now they couldn't – they needed the money, and besides there was nowhere for them to go, and the thought of leaving their apartment to the Nazis – to Valter Kroeling in particular – was nauseating.

Despite the risks – despite the fact that it made no sense to risk so much for so little – in the end it was the way she'd felt that day in the park, her eyes shining, the gentle summer breeze stirring her hair, that feeling that at last here was something that made life feel worthwhile again, that made up her mind to join.

She left with Clotilde in the middle of the night, dressed in black, and together with a few of the girls she'd gone to school with, they painted signs of resistance on the city's walls. She came home just before dawn, her heart racing, yet her spirits high. It made dealing with Valter Kroeling more bearable, somehow. When she found black paint beneath her fingers, despite all her scrubbing, she clenched them together like a secret badge of honour.

'Just be careful,' whispered her papa on the second night, when she slipped back inside with the dawn. She clutched her heart in fright as his greying head appeared at the stairs. 'Clotilde… well, she's never been able to do anything by halves, you know that.'

'It will be fine, Papa. She won't do anything to get us caught.'

It was true: it was a well-oiled operation. Clotilde knew the schedules of all the German officers stationed in their arrondissement, knew when they were taking a break, where they liked to hide in wait. She was like a cat, prowling the city late at night.

Mireille didn't ask how he knew where they'd been. She knew that he had his own spies.

He looked at her now, shook his head. 'I don't like it. I heard that they're starting to punish the ones they find – are a few painted messages worth your life?'

She felt her body go cold at his words. He sighed. 'I'm doing everything I can' – his voice broke slightly, the sound tearing at her heart – 'just to hold it together with them here in the day – and now you're doing this at night?' The disappointment in his eyes was too much to bear. She knew he was right. But still, he just didn't understand.

'I have to do something, Papa. Or I'll go mad.'

His face softened slightly. 'I wish you wouldn't,' was all he said. Which was worse than if he had shouted. He didn't forbid her to go. Perhaps it would have been better if he had. All she felt as a result was torn.

CHAPTER THIRTEEN

Mireille hated to admit it, but her father was right. Clotilde had become reckless. Even she could see that now. Now that her friend had graduated in recent weeks from scribbling messages of resistance on the walls of the city late at night to delivering messages, secret correspondence from the network of the higher ranks of the resistance, who'd heard about her. Messages that helped spread the word about attacks planned on the officers, helping captured soldiers escape, forging documents. If these were found, she would be killed. There was no doubt about it.

Mireille worried about her, because she'd started taking too many chances. Before, there had always been someone keeping watch. Someone stationed who would warn them, help them stay out of sight before they were caught. At first Clotilde was out one or two nights a week, when Mireille joined her, but now it was all night, all day. How long would it be before she was captured?

'This is more than just scribbles on walls now,' Clotilde had explained one night when the rain battered the rooftops, muffling her voice, as Mireille stood on the stairs after midnight, waiting for her friend to come home. An echo of the warning she'd received from her father a few weeks before.

Clotilde's dark eyes were alight when she entered the shop, and they shone when they saw Mireille waiting. There was no Star of David pinned to her lapel any more. If the Nazis saw that, she'd be sent to prison for sure.

'Clotilde, I'm worried. It's too much. You need to scale back. Please.'

Her friend shook her dark red curls. Squared her broad shoulders. 'More people are joining now. There's this man… de Gaulle, he sends secret radio broadcasts. That's what I was doing tonight. Just listening. Listening to all that they have planned – how we are going to get our country back from the inside out. We're so close now, Mireille. We will get rid of them, if we work together. First, though, we've got to fight this fear that they've made us feel – they're making us think we are weaker than we are, with these stupid curfews… because they know that's when we will strike back, and we will,' she said, slamming a sizeable fist into her palm. 'You'll see. Trust me.'

Mireille nodded. She wanted to, more than anything. Every day the Nazis took away small parts of everyone's dignities, imposing curfews, rations and rules – rules that now meant that her best friend was no longer 'acceptable'. It was unthinkable; she was the bravest person she knew.

Mireille woke up the next morning tired, her stomach grumbling from hunger. It was a new state of affairs. The rations that the Nazis had put them on meant that some days there just wasn't enough to go around between her, her father and Clotilde – who as a Jew got even less. Combined with the stress of having the Nazis constantly inside the shop, her hunger meant that she was now always stressed, always on edge, and it showed.

The army doctor, Mattaus Fredericks, returned to the Gribouiller six weeks after he'd first ordered his medical dictionary from the shop. As time had passed he'd found that the book he'd ordered wasn't quite as necessary any more – he'd had to learn medical French fast these past few months. Pain only spoke one language, after all. Still, when the young Mademoiselle Mireille from the bookstore called to tell him his book was there, he decided to come and get it anyway, mostly so that he could see her face again. There wasn't much to brighten his days at the hospital, and he looked forward to seeing the pretty young bookseller more than he'd like to admit.

When he walked inside, his eyes fell on her sitting behind a large desk, where she was shuffling piles of paperwork. He cleared his throat to get her attention. She looked up with a pained frown and he was shocked to see the change in her from their first meeting. Her large blue eyes had lost their sparkle, and the silvery sheen was less prominent in her shoulder-length blonde hair. Her skin was almost grey. She was still beautiful, but looked ever so slightly washed out, like a watercolour painting.

'Ah, Herr Doctor,' she said, getting up to fetch the dictionary, which she'd placed on a nearby shelf with the other orders. He was memorable with his vivid green eyes, dark blond hair and large, muscular frame.

He stared at her. She seemed thinner. 'Are you quite well, mademoiselle? You look a little pale, unhappy.'

She straightened and her mouth fell open slightly, in apparent disbelief at his words. Her blue eyes snapped in sudden fire. She stepped closer in her anger, her hand balled into a fist at her side.

'Unhappy? Are you honestly questioning why I look unhappy?'

Her gaze moved from him to the other side of the store, and its clutch of Nazi officers in the corner, busy with the printing press.

He sucked air in through his teeth. Her voice was low – only he could hear her response, but it was chilling, and he regretted the question instantly.

Mireille blew out her cheeks. 'Sometimes you Germans ask a little too much. Is it not enough that you are *here*? It is surely beggaring belief that we must be happy about it.' She made a small sound of derision, then continued, attempting to pull herself together: 'Can you settle for polite? It's all I have, and that, too, is wearing a little thin these days – less food tends to do that.'

She thrust the book at him and forced a very fake smile. 'Good day,' she said, dismissing him.

He made no move to leave. Reaching inside for his wallet, he said, 'I haven't paid yet.'

A muscle flexed in her jaw, and she said, 'Forget it.'

'I insist,' he said, putting the money on the table.

Still he did not leave.

Mireille ground her teeth as he stood staring at her, peering at her with more than a little concern.

'Can I help you with something else?' she asked, barely managing to keep herself together. Despite all the lectures she gave her dear papa, the truth was she had inherited at least a little of his temper.

'Have you got enough to eat?' he asked. 'Iron deficiencies in women are common, especially if the food is being rationed. Choose wisely, and make sure you eat green vegetables, meat, and get enough rest.'

Her eyes widened. 'Rest? How can I rest here, M'sieur – when your men are always here, always.'

As if on cue, and perhaps to defend what he considered his territory, Valter Kroeling stepped inside the shop, which had been relatively peaceful that morning with the officer out of the way. He eyed Mireille and the doctor, then greeted him with a salute, 'Herr Stabsarzt Fredericks,' though his watery pale eyes seemed to flash with something like suspicion.

'Kroeling.'

'Mam'selle,' drawled Kroeling, turning to her, revealing his pointed teeth in the rat-like smile that always chilled her heart. 'We must go over the new order – there are some books on it that have now been banned.' He gave the doctor a thin smile. 'I wouldn't want the young lady and her father to get into any trouble,' he explained to Fredericks, who to his obvious annoyance hadn't moved away.

'So you have set up the press here,' said Fredericks, turning to Kroeling, his brow raised, and Kroeling nodded.

'I thought that it was decided that these premises were too small.'

'It suits us fine,' said Kroeling, a frown deepening between his brows. 'Besides, the location makes it perfect for distribution of our pamphlets.'

As a senior medical officer, Fredericks had the right to enquire and suggest improvements; particularly if it impacted the health and safety of the army, and suggestions along these lines couldn't be ignored, especially if it was in the interest of the Reich.

Fredericks looked at the men all cramped together in their half of the shop, sharing one big table covered with stacks of magazines and newsletters. The small press took up most of the room, along with the typewriters and assembled company. It looked and felt crowded and noisy.

'It is causing the family some stress. I would recommend that other premises be considered. It looks… cramped. Inefficient…'

Fire flared in Kroeling's eyes at the insult, but he held his tongue.

'Perhaps we can make more room then by taking over the whole shop – we had thought to be kind by leaving the family their business. Surely no business at all would be more *stressful*.'

Fredericks's face was impassive. 'Yes, you could do that, but even then the space would be far too small, and this is a perfectly good bookshop in the centre of Paris, serving a lot of people. I would not like to have to file a report that this operation looks less than efficient – haphazard, even.'

It was that word that was perhaps the deal-breaker.

'Perhaps an easier solution would be to move to headquarters, but to store some of the pamphlets here for ease of distribution due to its good location, as you say – that might be a fair compromise.'

Kroeling looked murderous, but he inclined his head. The word 'haphazard' applied to his work would be fatal, and he knew it.

'We will do as you suggest. However, as the manager of the bookshop, appointed by Herr Brassling' – Brassling was a group captain, and outranked Fredericks – 'I will ensure that I visit regularly,' he assured Mireille, his eyes dark, blaming her for this. His expression made it clear that he felt she had said something to the doctor about the situation, or else he never would have interfered. 'Particularly since some books seem to have been ordered that shouldn't.'

Fredericks nodded. 'That sounds acceptable.'

He looked at Mireille, who stared back in surprise. Had this man, whom she'd just insulted, somehow managed to make one of her dreams – less time with these Nazis and their magazine, and Valter Kroeling in particular – come true?

She knew better than to thank him, but she did give him the first real smile she'd given anyone in a long time, particularly when Kroeling started barking out orders for his men to start moving their things to the German headquarters, some five miles away.

CHAPTER FOURTEEN

After he came for his dictionary, Mattaus Fredericks popped into the Gribouiller every week. He always bought a book, but she knew, in the way that all women seem to know these things, that really he came to see her. He checked up on her, as though she were one of his patients.

Occasionally he brought extra fruit and vegetables, and sometimes even meat. When Mireille made to refuse the gifts, he told her that they were surplus to the hospital. 'They over cater for us – the food is measured on a two-hundred-bed facility. Most days we don't make that number, and so there is too much food, food that will go to waste. I thought perhaps you could use it, rather than have us throw it away… but if you'd prefer I can—'

'No, it is fine, we will take it, thank you.'

Mireille was proud, and a large part of her wanted to refuse the doctor's gifts, but the fact was, Clotilde could count every one of her ribs, and she herself had gone down a dress size, despite the fact that she had been slim to begin with. They could use the food, no matter where it came from.

Mattaus was gratified in the weeks that followed to see the colour return to her cheeks, and the strain lessen about her eyes, now that she was getting better nutrients, and she was no longer under the constant watchful gaze of Valter Kroeling.

Despite Mattaus's interference, though, it hadn't stopped Kroeling from visiting several times a week, but now that he was no longer based in the bookshop all day, Mireille felt for the first time in months as if she might actually be able to breathe.

Her father was also finally able to resume his work – as there was less chance of him losing his temper and getting himself jailed now that the printing press was no longer based in their small shop.

However, days later, everything changed. Mattaus came inside at the same moment as Valter Kroeling, the latter saying, 'I see you are back again, Herr Stabsarzt. I am surprised that you favour this bookshop, as there is one much closer to the hospital.'

The doctor managed a polite smile, and said, 'There is – alas, it is not as good, or as well supplied.'

Another Nazi officer looked from the doctor to Mireille, who was busy adding some new stock to the shelves, and raised an eyebrow. 'Perhaps it is something else that draws the doctor here.'

One of Kroeling's men laughed, and joked, 'Perhaps it's the bistro that operates as a brothel around the corner.'

The doctor turned to look at the man, who seemed to remember his manners fast. 'I apologise, Captain.'

'Good.'

When Kroeling and his men left, Mireille asked the doctor, 'Why did they call you Captain?' She was curious, was all. Curious about the man that Kroeling seemed to both hate and respect, and curious that somehow, as a result her life had improved, though she didn't want to be too grateful for the presence of a Nazi officer in her life – she couldn't be sure if he expected something in return for his kindness, and didn't want to find herself narrowly escaping the flame only to find herself facing a fire instead.

'Because, while I am a doctor, I am also a captain.'

She nodded. It didn't exactly make her feel any better that her new 'friend' was a high-ranking Nazi. It didn't make her feel better at all.

The other problem with having Mattaus Fredericks come calling into the shop so frequently was that Kroeling noticed. Perhaps the young man saw this as a challenge. The unfortunate result was that the temporary relief she'd enjoyed from his constant presence soon came to an end, and he began to visit more frequently as a result, sometimes twice a day. Even after the store was officially closed, she would find him there, waiting by the door.

This new arrangement was particularly dangerous for Clotilde.

While she was careful to disguise herself whenever she undertook a mission, seeing Valter Kroeling by the apartment, and knowing that he was now watching the store at odd hours, meant that she had to be even more careful.

'Just scale it back, for now,' warned Mireille. 'It's too much of a risk.'

Clotilde's face was angry. 'That's what they want – for us to feel defeated. To feel like we have no choice but to stop fighting, to give in. I won't let them win.'

Mireille shook her head. She was tired. Sick of all the games, the politics, the manoeuvres. 'Haven't they already?'

Clotilde shook her head. 'No, not yet.'

Clotilde had convinced Mireille to use the bookshop as one of the areas where they could deliver the resistance's secret correspondence. It was simple to slip a note in a book, and hand it over to one of the members, always a woman, wearing a red scarf. She would pocket the note, to pass on to Clotilde in the evening. Mireille had done a few of these exchanges over the past weeks. Each time it gave her a thrill to know that she was doing it beneath the noses of Valter Kroeling and even Mattaus Fredericks. But now that Kroeling was making it a habit to appear at odd hours, showing up whenever she least expected it, it simply wasn't safe any more. 'We can't go on, Clotilde. Not here. You've seen how he watches us – he will figure it out.'

Clotilde nodded, and Mireille breathed a sigh of relief – one that was not destined to last. Her friend squared her shoulders. 'I'll just have to find another place for the exchanges – I can't stop, not now.'

'I wish you would. It's getting dangerous – ever more so, 'specially for you.'

Mireille was referring to the growing animosity that the Germans were displaying to the Jews.

Clotilde nodded. 'That's why I have to keep fighting, don't you see?'

It was nearing curfew when Valter Kroeling showed up at the bookshop door in mid-autumn, a week later, drunk. He let himself into the store with the key he'd had made, while she was busy tidying up. She swallowed, seeing him there while she was alone, and he gave her a leering grin as he staggered inside, giving a low bone-chilling whistle when he saw her, evidently happy to find her by herself.

'I wondered if I would ever get you alone, *Fräulein*,' he said, his pencil-moustachioed lips quivering, his needle-like teeth glistening with spittle into a chilling smile.

Mireille's heart started to thud. She shot a glance up the stairs to where her father had gone. 'I'm afraid, Herr Leutnant Kroeling, that the store is now closed. I was just shutting up for the night, before heading to bed.'

Kroeling's smile widened. 'Is that an invitation?'

She swallowed, took a step back. 'No, I am sorry – I meant I am going upstairs. My father—'

'He can wait for you, surely? This won't take long,' he said. Before she knew it she was seized in his arms and his face was inches from hers, his breath sour with the scent of stale whisky and cigarettes, which met her nostrils like an assault as he bent her roughly towards him for a kiss.

'No!' she screeched. 'Please, let me go.'

He laughed, and squeezed her even tighter, his hold crushing, suffocating. It was designed to show one thing only – how much stronger than her he was.

'You have teased me long enough. Playing me against your doctor – I thought perhaps that you were his, but I have checked to make sure and I see that I was mistaken.'

'I am,' declared Mireille. 'I am with the doctor,' she said suddenly, fear in her eyes, in her heart, seizing upon the lie like a life raft.

'No, *Fräulein*, he has denied it. He does not come here, except in the day for his books. You, I think, belong only to me – I think even he understands this,' he said. Then his eyes went dark, menacing, and his mouth slammed into hers, rough and hard. She struggled against him, feeling as if she might gag as his tongue entered her mouth, hot and rank, tasting of old liquor and something else that was all him, oily and vile. She pushed against him, kicking and thrashing, and tearing at his skin for freedom, when he at last let her go. She gasped for air and he slapped her hard and she fell against the wooden floor. The room began to swim and she saw stars, the blood rushing to her ears, and she staggered towards the door on her hands and feet. He grabbed her by her ankle, pulling her backwards with force, her nails scraping along the wooden floor as she cried out, tears pooling in her ears. He hefted his body on top of hers, his eyes gleaming in victory. He put a hand over her mouth to stop her screams, and then fiddled with his trousers, lifting her skirt up while she howled.

Then, suddenly, there was a loud crack, and the heavy weight of Kroeling was gone. Heart jackhammering in her chest, she looked up through the haze of fog from her tears. She saw her father's face, and the blood on his hands. 'Papa,' she breathed. 'What have you done?'

CHAPTER FIFTEEN

Mireille inched over to Valter Kroeling's body to check if he was still breathing. He was face down, and there was blood on the wooden floor. She was shaking as she put her ear to his lips. She was praying, too. She heard the slow rhythm of his breathing and fell back onto her haunches, closing her eyes, rocking back and forth, sobs catching at her throat. Her father rushed forward to embrace her, kneeling on the floor and enfolding her in his arms.

She put her head on his shoulder, breathing in his comforting, familiar smell, and the sobs came harder.

'It's okay now,' said Vincent, 'he won't hurt you.'

She shook her head, gasping for air, her chin wobbling. 'It's not that, Papa. What will they do to you when they find out what you did?'

He looked at her in disbelief, his blue eyes fierce. 'He tried to *rape* you in my own house. I was defending *my daughter* – they must understand that, must see that I was just protecting you. Besides, he was drunk, out of his mind.'

She shook her head. She wished he was right, but after having been subjected to these Nazi officers all day, she knew better now. 'Oh, Papa, they will never blame him for that, never, not without a witness – a German witness,' she amended. 'They would never take our word.'

Which was when he looked at her and for the first time realised how quickly she had had to grow up, and just how terrifying and awful that fact truly was.

Mireille and her father moved Valter Kroeling into the small storeroom downstairs, and barricaded the door. Vincent insisted that when he woke up and there was an inquiry to be faced, he would tell the truth, though perhaps even he knew the chance for him to escape the firing squad was slim at best. Which was why he came up with a plan.

In the morning, he paid a young boy to deliver a message for the doctor, Mattaus Fredericks, to come quickly.

When Mattaus came, Vincent raised a finger to his lips and took him to the storeroom where Valter Kroeling was lying, spread-eagled and fast asleep on the floor, a large purpling bruise covering one eye. His mouth was open while he snored, the stench of stale alcohol strong and repugnant. Mattaus bent to examine him, his nose wrinkling at the smell.

'It looks like he was knocked out.'

Dupont nodded. 'That's because he was – by me.'

Mattaus raised a brow and Dupont said, 'I did it when I found him trying to force himself on my daughter.'

The doctor's eyes flashed in anger. Then he stood up, indicating for Dupont to follow him.

'He tried to rape Mireille?'

Dupont nodded. 'Yes. Last night.'

'He was unsuccessful?'

Dupont closed his eyes. He didn't like to admit how close a thing it was. If he hadn't been upstairs… if he hadn't heard the thuds downstairs…

'He didn't get that far.'

The doctor sighed in relief.

'Look, when he wakes up – it's probably all over for me. I know that,' said Dupont. 'I know what they do to people who go against them and he's not a reasonable man… this is not about me. I sent for you, because I think that in your own way you care for my daughter. Kroeling told her before he tried to rape her last night that he had stayed away only because he thought there was a chance that she was your "woman". While I do not wish for you to misunderstand me, and I do not wish for you to make such a thing happen, I would like you to look out for her if possible, if I am killed.'

The doctor nodded. 'I will look after her, I assure you. But surely it will not come to that.'

Mattaus woke Valter Kroeling with a bucket of ice water. Kroeling startled awake, groaning and staggering as he tried to stand, then sat back down. His hands went to his bloodstained head, felt the lump that had formed on his forehead, and his face grew angry as the night's activities came rushing forward in his memory. 'I am going to kill that old man, with my bare hands! I should have done it on my first day here!' His fists balled at his sides, and he lurched forward, screaming and threatening. Mattaus laid a heavy hand on his shoulder. The doctor was a large, imposing figure, and Kroeling stopped, seeing Mattaus's face, which was cold.

'You will have a hard time doing that while I'm here, I'm afraid, not after what you did.'

'What I did?' Valter Kroeling looked blank. Then his eyes grew dark and he sneered. 'Ah, the bitch – I suppose she fed you some lie, and you believed her?'

'I did.'

'Well then you are a fool.'

'And you are a rapist.'

Kroeling's eyes flashed. 'Or just a lover. Have you ever stopped to wonder that maybe that innocent act of hers is just that – an act?'

Mattaus gritted his teeth. 'Get out of this shop right now. Go and sleep it off. That's an order.'

Kroeling rubbed his head and turned to leave, but before he left he spat: 'That old man can't just strike an officer and get away with it…'

The doctor sighed. 'I said, go.'

Kroeling's lips curled. 'This isn't over.'

It was a warning, Mattaus knew. When he was gone Mattaus muttered, 'No. It isn't.' He was angry, and he felt out of control; it wasn't a good place to be.

They came for Dupont that afternoon. Kroeling's men had her father taken away in handcuffs and beaten, while Mireille screamed and howled.

For now he was to be sent to jail only. It appeared that Mattaus had managed to convince them that incarceration would be the best option for a father who thought his daughter was being raped and acted in her defence.

Mireille followed them to the jail, begging and pleading, but her pleas fell on deaf ears. When she arrived back at the apartment, her heart skipped a beat in fear to find that there was someone inside. She entered with her heart in her throat, to find a man's suitcase and a box of belongings next to the stairs. She picked up a small statue of the Virgin Mary that rested on the shelf, and went up the stairs. If Kroeling was here, then she would fight – resistance or death, she decided. She wouldn't let him finish what he'd started the night before.

As she entered the apartment, her eyes widened instead to find the doctor sitting on the sofa, waiting for her.

'What are you doing here?' she demanded, in shock.

He tucked in his bottom lip for a moment as if not sure where to begin. 'I am moving in.'

She gasped. 'You're – *what*?'

He stood up and her knees went weak: could this really be happening again? He was so tall and *big*. He had seemed gentle in a way, despite his size, but maybe not. Were all the men here mad, primal beings?

He held up his hands as she clutched the statue, as if ready to use it as a weapon.

'I am here for your protection only.'

She frowned, lowering the weapon slightly. 'My protection?'

'Yes – your father—'

'I do not need protecting from my father.'

He gave a half grin that revealed very even teeth. 'Of course not. What I am saying is that your father spoke to me—'

'He spoke to you?'

'He told me what happened last night. He worried that if he were taken it would happen again.' He looked away, not meeting her eyes. 'He told me what Kroeling said, what he tried to do – and how it might have been prevented. How Kroeling had at first stayed away because he thought you might be… mine.'

Mireille bit her lip. 'I do not want to be your woman,' she said, unconsciously using the words that Kroeling had taunted her with. She felt her stomach twist, and the tears fall. It was just too much, after everything that had already happened.

He took a step back. 'I would not ask – I am not asking now. I will not force…' He stopped, swallowed, then attempted in vain to clarify himself. 'I am here, as I said, for your protection. May I use the room at the end of the apartment?'

Mireille stared at him. It was a question, not an order. At last his words seemed to penetrate – he wanted to stay to protect her from Kroeling. Of course, with her father away, there was every chance he would come back and attempt to finish what he'd started. Her knees grew weak. She felt the air leave her chest in sudden gratitude. It was the smallest room, and held only a child's wardrobe.

'Yes,' she said. 'I –' She cleared her throat. 'Thank you. I'm sorry for what I said.'

He raised a hand, dismissing her words, and nodded. 'I will say goodnight now, then. Please call if you need me.'

And she watched him go, not knowing what to say. Hating that he was here, hating how grateful she was that he was, and hating most of all that because of people like him, she was in this situation in the first place.

CHAPTER SIXTEEN

1962

'Dupont was arrested?' said Valerie in shock. 'For defending his daughter?'

Madame Joubert nodded, her eyes sad. 'He had struck an officer, badly wounded him – they didn't see it from the other side. What Dupont had done was enough to have him executed. The fact that he wasn't was because the other officer – the doctor – had intervened on Mireille's behalf, and even then, he was sent to jail for four months.'

Valerie shook her head. 'What a crazy world that was. I can't even imagine it.'

Madame Joubert nodded, her eyes thoughtful as she watched Valerie put the photograph back in Dupont's desk, and said, 'Well, for that, at least, I am glad.'

Valerie inclined her head, but the woman shook hers.

'Tell me, *chérie*, when are you going to tell him?'

Valerie frowned. 'Pardon?'

Madame Joubert's hand was still on her shoulder, gentle despite her considerable size. Her dark eyes were knowing, and she picked up a strand of Valerie's hair, and ran it through her fingers.

'When are you going to tell him who you really are?'

Valerie turned pale, her eyes wide.

'You *are* Mireille's child, aren't you?'

Valerie's heart began to thud loudly in her ears. She bit her lip, then, very slowly, as if she were finally letting go of something heavy, something that had felt like a weight about her neck, she nodded.

It was then, as Madame Joubert gasped, and slipped into deep, silent sobs that racked her large body from the inside out, a hand clutching the desk as her knees seemed about to give out, that Valerie realised that the woman hadn't known. Not really. She had only hoped.

Valerie left Dupont a message that she would be returning later, and not to worry about dinner for her. She opened a tin of tuna for the cat and telephoned Freddy, telling him that she'd see him the following night.

She'd gone with Madame Joubert next door, helping her inside, the older woman's fingers shaking, the tears coursing unstopped down her cheeks, while Valerie got her up the stairs to her small two-bedroom apartment, where she poured them each a glass of wine, wishing that there was something stronger.

'B-but how?' said Madame Joubert, when she'd at last caught her breath. She clutched at Valerie's hand as if it were a balloon, as if she were afraid that she would float away.

'How what?' said Valerie with a frown, as she sat next to her on the forest green sofa, sinking into the plush velvet cushions.

Madame Joubert's eyes were wide; the kohl had spooled beneath them in inky smears. Valerie had never seen the glamorous woman look so vulnerable, so fragile.

Madame Joubert stared at her, shaking her head. 'How are you here? How did you find us?'

'My aunt – Mireille's cousin, Amélie, she told me, told me about my grandfather, when I turned twenty. She thought I had a right to know.'

Madame Joubert shook her head again. 'Oh, Amélie,' she whispered. 'What have you done?'

Valerie felt her cheeks turn red in anger. 'I did have a right to know, even if he didn't – doesn't want me in his life. I had a right to know that he was alive, and why he gave me away.'

Madame Joubert laid her confused dark eyes on Valerie. 'Doesn't want you – is that what Amélie told you?' She shook her head. 'You mean, after she told you he was alive she didn't tell you why you were taken to live with her?'

It was Valerie's turn to look confused. 'She said that my grandfather gave me away, that he didn't want to be in my life, that he'd said it would be best for me to think that he was dead. Aunt Amélie thought – when I was old enough – at least, that's what she said, that I had a right to know.'

On the day Valerie had been told, she'd found her aunt sitting on her bed, looking out at the garden of their north London house below, the sky turning to blush.

Downstairs the music was still going. Someone had put on the Beatles, and Freddy was doing his best John Lennon impersonation.

She'd taken her presents upstairs – books and jumpers and notebooks from friends and family who knew her so well – when she saw Aunt Amélie sitting there alone. Her face was unusually sombre, a frown between her eyes.

'Are you all right?' asked Valerie, worried, putting her presents on the chair, and wondering why she was sitting there in the near dark.

Amélie nodded. She took a deep breath, as if she were gathering her courage. 'I'm fine. Come and take a seat.'

Valerie did.

In her aunt's hand was the small photograph of her mother that Valerie kept always in a frame by her bed. Valerie looked at it, but didn't say anything. It was unlike her aunt to ever speak about her mother – usually when Valerie tried, she'd change the subject.

'I have been thinking about your mother, Mireille. We grew up far away from each other. She in Paris. Me in Haute-Provence – in the mountains. Anyway, she was my cousin, and I loved her, even though we never got to see each other as much as we would have liked.'

Valerie took the photograph. It had been a long time since she'd really looked at the black-and-white image, seen her *mother* sitting there, instead of a young woman with a cat and a smiling face.

'I think it is time I told you the truth.'

Valerie's heart skipped a beat. The air was tense. 'What do you mean?'

Amélie sighed, and put the photograph back on the side table. 'Your grandfather, Vincent, is still alive.'

'I have a grandfather?' Valerie was shocked. Amélie had always told her that there was no one left. *No one*. Apart from her, that was.

'Yes, it was he who gave you to me, after your mother died. He wanted me to take you away from the war, from Paris.'

'He gave me to you?' cried Valerie, trying to process this. Not understanding. 'He wanted me to be safe?'

'Yes… and no, he wanted you to grow up away from France. Away from the war. He wanted you to have a better home. But he also thought it would be better if you thought that he was dead, easier for you somehow.'

Valerie blinked. Her aunt's words were like glass: everywhere she turned, they seemed capable of cutting. He was the only direct family she had – and he hadn't wanted her? 'He wanted me to think he was dead?'

'Yes.'

'Why? Why did he hate me?'

Amélie closed her eyes. 'It wasn't hate. Don't think that, please. I think he cared for you in his own way. He just couldn't keep you.'

'Did he need to make you lie, then – if he did it for my good?'

'Maybe he thought you would go looking for him one day.'

'Why wouldn't he want me to?'

Amélie shook her head. 'Only he could tell you that.'

Madame Joubert took a sip of her wine, and shook her head. 'But she didn't tell you the right thing. I think it would kill Dupont to know that you thought that he didn't want you.' Her voice caught, and she closed her eyes. 'It was the exact opposite.'

Valerie blinked, hope fluttering in her chest. She swallowed, but still tears smarted in her eyes. 'I don't think that can be true – if he had wanted me, then why didn't he send for me after the war was over?'

Madame Joubert blew out her cheeks, as if she was trying to find the courage to say what she needed to say. 'Because, child – the war was never going to be over, not for you. Not if you stayed here in Paris.'

CHAPTER SEVENTEEN

1940

It was early November and Mireille couldn't sleep knowing that there was a Nazi sleeping not two hundred feet away from her.

She worried about her father, and Clotilde, whom she hadn't seen for three days.

Every sound was amplified in the darkness. Every creak a bullet, every shadow a man with a knife. When dawn broke, there were deep welt-like shadows beneath her eyes, which were swollen and red from her tears.

When she went to the kitchen, dressed in her robe, her feet bare and cold against the polished hardwood floors, her heart jolted in fear to find the large form of Mattaus standing in the shadows.

He turned to her, a furrow between his brows at her small gasp. 'I startled you – I'm sorry. I thought I would put the coffee on,' he said, pointing at the cafetière, and getting a mug for her from the cabinet. It was such a simple thing, a small act of domesticity that seemed even more personal, and invasive in a way. Even Kroeling had never entered their kitchen before. She hadn't imagined him being here, a place that, even during the worst of the past few months, had been a refuge without her realising – till now.

Mireille closed her eyes for a moment. A part of her wanted to scream, to shout, and tell him to get out of her kitchen, her house, her life. But she took the mug from his outstretched hand, then breathed out. The truth was she knew that she should be grateful to him – because if he was here, it meant that Valter Kroeling was not, and at least the doctor, despite being German, despite being a Nazi, had not forgotten what it meant to be a gentleman, for the time being at least.

'Thank you,' she whispered. She didn't mean for the coffee, and perhaps he knew that, because he said, 'It's what I would want someone to have done for my sister, Greta. She's three years younger than me, a schoolteacher – she hates this,' he said, looking away, his green eyes seeming sad.

Mireille frowned. 'Hates what?'

'The war. We've already lost one brother to it.'

She looked up at him, realising, for the first time perhaps, that for the other side there were women like her who were losing their fathers and brothers, who wished nothing more than for the fighting to stop. She swallowed. 'I hate it too.' Her eyes felt as if they were filled with glass, as if she had aged a hundred years overnight. She looked away from his pitying gaze.

'You look exhausted.'

She sighed. 'I couldn't sleep.'

'Your father will be all right. They won't mistreat him – I have made sure of that.'

She took another shuddery breath, and offered him a small smile. 'M'sieur Fredericks, thank you, this family is grateful to you.'

'Though it would prefer not to have to be.'

There was a ghost of a laugh in Mireille's mouth. 'Yes, I cannot deny that.'

The small clearing of her features, showing the young girl beneath her pain and suffering, touched his heart. He set the mug down on the kitchen table. 'I'm leaving now – I need to get to the hospital. I will return this evening at around six.'

'You don't need to tell me your plans,' said Mireille with a frown.

He straightened, his green eyes warm. 'I only tell you so that later you will not be startled.'

She closed her eyes. Yes, that made sense. It was a kindness he was offering. It was strange to think of someone like him as kind. She wondered if it was dangerous too.

He put a set of brass keys down on the table. 'These are the new keys to the shop and the apartment – I changed the locks last night. My father was a locksmith in Lorraine,' he said.

That explained the noises she'd heard in the middle of the night, as if someone were breaking in – he'd been trying to prevent that very thing.

'Keep the doors locked. Kroeling – despite my best efforts to have him tried – is still a free man, though he is no longer in charge of the press, as it is believed that he was neglecting his duties.'

Mireille was shocked. 'So he won't be coming here any more.'

Fredericks shrugged. 'Not in an official capacity, I am sure, but what I do know is that a man like him won't be pleased at what has happened, and I worry that he will seek his revenge, not on me, but on you.' His jaw flexed. 'So, please keep the doors locked, especially at night.'

The prison was overflowing. There was the stench of unwashed bodies, disease and desperation. Rationing was having its effects, and here in the jail, many of the city's poorest souls, who had been forced to try to come to terms with something they could not, had been living hand to mouth, trying to fight an army of guns and tanks with knives and handmade weapons. It was they who were the ones paying the highest price.

Despite all her pleas, despite using Mattaus's name, they wouldn't let Mireille see her father.

A dour-faced officer was busy with a mountain of paperwork – German efficiency at its best – adding ever more names to a never-ending list of traitors, Parisians who would never be free again. He looked bored and well fed, and barely looked up at her.

'No visitors.'

'Please.'

His face was immobile, and he carried on filling out his list.

'Please, M'sieur, my father needs me. I am worried about him. Can I see him, just for a moment?'

'No,' said the guard, his face impassive. 'He has committed a crime.'

Mireille felt her heart sink into her feet. 'Can you give him a message, please?'

'No messages.'

She closed her eyes. He hadn't even bothered to look at her. Her fingers balled into fists as a group of Nazi officers filed past her, each eyeing her appreciatively. She swallowed her frustration and left the prison, her shoulders stooped.

When she got back to the apartment, she saw a thin man with dark hair waiting outside the shop. He seemed to be looking in through the window, peering into the glass. He was French, down on his luck – judging by the state of his clothes and his demeanour.

'Can I help you?'

He looked at her, then straightened up, his face hardening slightly. He looked scruffy, as if he hadn't bathed or shaved in days. 'You the bookshop brat?'

She frowned at his rude tone. 'Excuse me?'

He smirked as he continued more politely, but sardonically, as if she were dim-witted: 'Your father owns this shop?'

'Yes.'

He snorted and scratched his head, looking at it. 'Must be nice,' he said, his dark eyes glittering with resentment, then spat close to her feet. 'To have a rich Nazi looking out for you. I see you put that pretty little body to good use. All right for some, isn't it?'

Her eyes widened, and she let out a small gasp. 'What?'

He sucked his teeth, giving her a look of pure loathing. 'Nothing.'

He looked down the street, then back up at her, daring to ask, 'You don't have any extra food in there, do you?'

'I don't.'

He swore, calling her a Nazi whore, before moving off to the other side of the street, where he lingered, his gaze never leaving hers.

Mireille stood for a moment, rooted to the spot as if she'd been slapped, then went to open the door to the bookshop, her fingers fumbling with the new keys, which she dropped on the pavement, her throat constricting. It was only when she'd locked the door again behind her, leaning her head against it, that she began to stop shaking.

The man was still there several hours later, across the street. It made her nervous. She wished he would go away. His dark eyes trailed her every move, with their mix of loathing and greed. It seemed that he'd stationed himself there, but for what reason, aside from trying to make her feel like some kind of traitor, Mireille couldn't say.

As a result, she hadn't even opened the bookshop for the day. Valter Kroeling and her father going to prison, not to mention the angry, homeless Frenchman across the street, all seemed combined to ensure that she felt like a trapped animal inside her own home.

CHAPTER EIGHTEEN

1962

Madame Joubert's words echoed in Valerie's head like a gunshot blast. 'The war would never be over. Not for you, not if you stayed.'

Valerie looked at her with a frown. 'What do you mean?'

She shook her head, and said, 'I just mean that your grandfather had his reasons – most of all he wanted to protect you.'

'Protect me from what? Knowing the truth about who I am, where I come from?'

Madame Joubert sighed, and put down her glass of wine. 'Yes, but it was more than that. You don't know – you haven't seen how they treat children like you here. It was for the best, trust me.'

Valerie slumped back against the sofa. Children like her? What did she mean? And then all at once it hit her, the truth, and what had been kept from her, why she'd been sent away. She doubled over, unable to breathe.

She saw stars, and for a moment, she thought she might be sick.

Through glazed eyes, with her head on her knees, she turned to Madame Joubert, who was crying again, and said the words, dragged the dark secret they had tried to keep from her out into the cold light of the apartment, where it slithered like a living thing with a poisonous sting. 'My father was *a Nazi*.'

And all Madame Joubert could do was nod, and then weep, along with her.

Valerie had left the apartment in a hurry after that, barely able to see where she was going through the haze of tears that fogged her eyes, her hands shaking uncontrollably, as the bedrock of who she was crumbled to dust before her feet. 'Don't tell M'sieur Dupont about who I am, please,' she'd said, before she went. 'Not yet. I want to know the rest, what happened to my mother – a-about my father.' She'd swallowed. 'You were her friend – her best friend. You owe her daughter that, please? Afterwards I will tell him.'

Madame Joubert had closed her eyes and nodded in the gloom, in defeat. 'All right.'

Valerie had taken a breath, then leant against the banner of the stairs. 'Thank you. I'll come back – I don't know when – to hear the rest, but tonight, I can't hear any more, I couldn't bear it.'

Madame Joubert had wiped her eyes; she looked drawn out herself. 'I understand.'

Valerie spent the rest of the evening walking the streets of Paris. It felt as if someone had thrown a grenade in her path and she was trying somehow to make her way out of the wreckage. She didn't take in much, didn't see the sights of Paris at night, lovers walking along the Pont Neuf, or the Eiffel Tower bathed in lights. Didn't hear the music from a jazz club, or the sound of laughter carried with the cool night air along the Seine.

Somehow, though she couldn't have explained how, or which streets she'd taken, or how long she'd walked, she found herself at Freddy's apartment. Her mascara ran in two deep rivers down her face. He opened the door in shock. He was still in a suit, his white shirt open at the throat, his dark hair sticking up all over the place. 'Val, love,' he said, seeing her face. 'What happened?'

She shook her head, and her face crumpled. 'I f-found out why they g-gave me away.'

He led her inside the apartment, then pulled her into a tight hug and whispered by her ear, 'They told you, then? About your father?'

She looked up at him, frowning. 'What?'

'That he was a German officer,' said Freddy. The word 'Nazi' was heavy in the air.

The air seemed to leave her lungs in a rush. 'You *knew*?'

He nodded. 'I guessed,' he said, not letting her leave his embrace, even as she struggled against him, tried to push – he was strong despite his wiry frame. 'But later, I looked it up. I'm a journalist,' he said, by way of defence.

She sank onto his small couch – it was sagging in the middle, the stuffing exposed like a bulging belly – and drank the glass of vodka he had poured her, which he'd put into his toothpaste mug as the rest of his dishes were piling up in the mouldy sink in the corner. It tasted slightly of peppermint.

'You *guessed*.' She repeated his words in disbelief. She had never imagined such a thing. Never. But now, sitting there, staring at the peeling green wallpaper, the stained mattress in the corner, and the small envelope of a window that overlooked a bistro, where jazz music could be heard even now at three a.m., she realised that it made sense, that guess. In retrospect.

He sat down next to her, but didn't say a word. His large brown eyes looked worried.

He hadn't been kidding: the apartment was undeniably a garret, and unbearable in general.

It was so horrid that despite her recent woes she couldn't block out how deeply, horribly awful it was. 'I can't believe you live here.'

He shrugged. 'Which is why I spend most of my time at the Cafe de Flore.'

She took another sip of the toothpaste-flavoured vodka, then nodded. 'Hemingway?'

'Hemingway,' he agreed.

The vodka began to have a slight numbing effect. She didn't smile, just shook her head and repeated, 'You knew. This whole time.'

'Not the whole time. But most of it, yes.'

She closed her eyes; she didn't know what she felt at that – betrayal? Anger? 'Why didn't you tell me?'

'I…' He hesitated. Then he moved closer to her, his hand touching her knee. 'I knew that this was how you'd take it – as if it meant something about *you*.'

She opened her eyes and frowned. 'Doesn't it? My father was a bloody *Nazi*. What does that make me?'

He shook his head, picked up her hand, and gave it a squeeze. 'It makes you, you. You're still the same person. I know they were following the most twisted, evil guy alive, but—'

'Don't do that, Freddy, just don't – just because this feels like hell, don't try and justify what they did.'

He ran a hand through his hair, which stuck up even more wildly. 'I won't, but don't go thinking that his choices are yours. And even then, you don't know what was in his soul – he might have been the nastiest guy alive, but that's not you, Val. I think, if it helps, you need to think of it as a cult: they were brainwashed… and not all of our guys were that great – they raped and pillaged too, I've come across some things, you know. I'm not excusing either, I promise you that, I'm just saying that it's not as black and white as we all like to make it out, and you shouldn't let it change how you feel about yourself.'

'Yeah,' said Valerie, 'but it does, though, doesn't it?' She wasn't sure how it couldn't help but change how she thought of herself. She finally understood now what Aunt Amélie had meant. She couldn't close that Pandora's box, not now after she'd opened it. She could understand now why Amélie hadn't wanted to tell her, why she'd said those words: 'Only he could tell you.' Only

Dupont. Amélie didn't want to be the one responsible for shattering everything Valerie knew about herself. For making her feel ashamed, somehow. She knew then in that moment how much this revelation would colour everything after.

She closed her eyes as she realised, 'Who could ever love me, knowing this about me?'

Freddy touched her face. 'I could.'

Tears slipped down her nose, and she opened her eyes to look at him, shaking her head. 'I mean, really love me.'

He smiled, his mouth soft. 'Yes.'

She sucked in air. 'Don't tease me, Freddy.' Her eyes were clouded with tears.

'I'm not teasing you.'

'Stop it,' she said, wiping her fingers beneath her eyes. She was getting angry now. To him this was always some game and she was tired of it. 'You know how I feel about you. You must have always known.' All her secrets were coming out now, and like a runaway train hurtling off the tracks, she couldn't stop it even if she tried. She was in full self-destruct mode.

'I always hoped that some day you could feel the same way, but now… how could you? Still to tease me about it…' She sniffed.

He looked at her, his dark eyes full of disbelief. 'Are you seriously this blind – about everything?'

She stared at him in confusion.

He gave a low laugh. 'Did you really think that I would choose to live *here* of all places if I didn't bloody love you?'

She looked at him, tears in her eyes. 'You were worried about me, that's what you said.'

He laughed. 'Yes. I was worried. You're my best friend.'

She closed her eyes in pain; it just kept coming tonight. 'I see.'

'I don't think you do. Which is kind of bonkers. Because the whole world seems to know except you.'

Then he kissed her.

She opened her eyes in shock, and he moved aside her curtain of hair, then laughed at her, in a gently teasing sort of way. 'You really can be the biggest idiot sometimes, you know that? There's never been anyone else, you twit. If I hadn't been in love with you since I was about nine, do you think I would have followed you here? And I don't care what you say, you're still you, Nazi father or not. It's never going to make a difference to how I feel about you, because that was him, not you.'

She thought about his other girlfriends. About how he always seemed to have a woman on the scene. 'But Freddy, there was always someone else. Some pretty girl… how could you have always loved me?'

He laughed again, and his fingers went to his hair, as though he were a little embarrassed. 'Call me old-fashioned but you were a bit young – I'm quite sure Amélie would have had me locked up if she knew how I felt about you… so, er, I had to look elsewhere, till you were old enough.' He cleared his throat. 'I'm still a bloke, what can I say?'

She grinned. It shouldn't have been funny or strangely sweet, except that it was, somehow, and soon their laughter turned into something else, as they began to kiss. Desire unfurled in her chest, raw and all-consuming, as she sank into it, her hands rough in his hair, pulling her to him as she sat on his lap. Freddy had never been Prince Charming, but then he had never pretended to be: he was real, and kind, and hers, at last.

CHAPTER NINETEEN

The bookshop cat had made himself at home on Valerie's bed, following her down to the shop every morning where she put out milk and food for him. Dupont, she could tell, hid his jealousy, but the cat was loyal to the man, and only ever slept during the daylight on his old, overstuffed chair, despite the smoke and the clutter.

Since she'd found out that her father was a Nazi, Valerie had become quiet, less prone to argue, less prone to much of anything, if truth be told. Her one source of joy and comfort was Freddy, though that had gone now too, temporarily at least, as he had been sent on an assignment to cover the new addition to the Berlin Wall. Since the wall dividing East from West had been put up overnight, in August the year before, to prevent the refugees fleeing, the story had made headlines: children, men and women being shot for trying to leave their own country. In early June, the second fence had been built further into East German territory, making it even harder for their citizens to leave. Already it had been called the Death Strip.

She'd always known that loving a political journalist wouldn't be easy, but this was the first time she'd ever truly worried about his safety. Telling herself that it was only for a few weeks didn't help. There was no arguing when you had entered the dark place, as Freddy liked to say.

'The good news,' he'd told her, while they lay in his small, sagging bed, sharing a cigarette, which he said made them rather

French indeed, 'is that after a few more assignments like this I'll probably be able to get a better apartment. Better pay.'

'Danger money,' she'd said, snuggling into his arms. Her green eyes looked worried.

And he'd shrugged, and agreed, 'Danger money,' and kissed the curve of her neck. No one got too close to that wall if they could help it.

Since they'd told each other how they felt, they had spent a lot of time together in Freddy's bed, making love and hiding out, creating a fortress from the world.

Freddy had come around and met Dupont shortly after they'd started dating officially. The two seemed to enjoy riling each other up; Freddy made a point of telling him how much he loved James Bond, which caused the old man to turn puce, and Dupont threatened to throw him out of the shop, especially when he insisted that they all go to watch the latest film. Instead, somehow, they ended up having a beer, and Freddy stayed for dinner. When Valerie had asked Dupont what he thought of Freddy after he left, he'd said, 'He needs a haircut, but you could do worse,' which was about as close to a nod of approval as she could ever have hoped for.

But now Freddy was gone, and all she had were her worries and the cat. She decided that beggars couldn't really be choosers, even if the cat stank of sardines.

Madame Joubert had come over the next day to see how she was, and they had spoken, though somewhat more stiffly than they had before. Gone, for now, was their easy conversation, the laughter, and the shared sympathy of dealing with the grouch that was Dupont.

It made little sense for Valerie to feel angry with her; keeping this secret had not been her idea, and neither had telling her, but there was a part of Valerie that was angry with her nonetheless.

She had been her mother's best friend – surely she could have said or done something to stop Dupont from giving her away, no matter how much pain he thought he was sparing her from.

'Come over tonight, *chérie*,' said Madame Joubert. 'Let's talk, all right?'

Valerie nodded.

'You are under the weather?' asked Dupont later that afternoon.

Valerie shook her head. 'No, I'm fine.'

He flung the copy of *Gigi* by Colette onto his messy table, muttering, 'Sentimental garbage.'

Valerie didn't respond. She just sighed, staring out the window at the cold late November day. Not really taking in what she saw, people walking past, their breath coming out in fog, tightly wrapped up in thick woollen scarves and coats. All she could think of was Freddy, in Berlin. And her father, a Nazi.

'Did you not hear what I said?'

Valerie let out a sigh. 'I heard you,' she said, as the cat, sensing her despair, came forward, rubbing himself along her bistro chair, and then jumping onto her lap, kneading Valerie's mustard corduroy skirt with its needle-like claws. 'You said it is sentimental drivel.'

He blinked. 'Last week you told me that if I didn't like Colette then I needed my head examined, and I should question my French blood. You made me read this,' he said, looking down at the book in despair. As if he would never get those few hours of his life back.

She sighed again. 'Yes.'

He frowned. 'Are the hours too long?'

She looked up. 'No. Why?'

'I was just checking. It's just you are not yourself lately.'

She stared. Dupont had noticed that she was out of sorts. Dupont. And he actually cared.

He got up, and she could hear him busy himself in the small downstairs kitchen where they kept a few mugs and a kettle.

After some time he came back with two mugs and a saucer full of rather boring-looking biscuits. Not his usual style of large chocolate-chip cookies.

He put the mugs down on the bistro table, then cleared his throat.

'What's this?' she asked, looking at the milky brown liquid.

He gave a deep sigh. 'It's that swill… you know, that horrible muck you like.'

She frowned in confusion, and then realisation dawned as she picked up the mug and gave it a sniff. 'M'sieur Dupont!' she exclaimed. 'Is this *tea*?'

He shrugged. '*Oui*. Don't make a fuss.'

She looked at it, then at him, in utter confusion.

Dupont had *theories* about tea. Mostly that it was awful, and that it stank, and he wouldn't keep any in the house. The only place that had been safe for her to drink a cup was in her bedroom.

She looked at the biscuits, then shook her head in amazement. They were Rich Tea biscuits: about as English as brollies and Marmite, and certainly not the sort of thing he'd ever buy himself. He must have gone to a special shop to buy these things for her. Though she couldn't imagine where they sold such things. He'd done it for her, because he had noticed that she looked sad, lost.

Dupont.

Tears pricked her eyes. She was touched more than she could say. But she knew he wouldn't appreciate a show, so she said, 'Thanks very much.' Then she took a bite of a biscuit and rallied, gave a deep sniff. 'M'sieur,' she said, as he turned to shuffle back to his desk with a grunt. 'You see that even the cat has given up on you because of your terrible taste in literature… honestly, to call Colette drivel… he is a French cat, after all.'

There was a small snort of amusement from Dupont, before he started grumbling, and saying that the closer we got to Christmas, people started to lose their minds, even mangy tail-less cats.

'He went to Madame Harvey for that tea – you know, the English woman who runs that little tea shop in the Rue des Arbres,' said a small, elfin-faced boy with dirty blond hair and thick lashes, some time later. 'I followed him.'

It was Henri, a young boy of around eleven or twelve, who sometimes earned a few francs from Dupont for doing odd jobs around the bookshop. His parents had fallen on hard times, and between Dupont and Madame Joubert they often found piecework for Henri, mainly to ensure that there was some food in his belly. He was a good sort, always ready to lend a hand, and Valerie had seen that he was interested in reading, so she set aside a few books for him every week, adventure stories mainly, that she thought he might like.

'Really?'

'*Oui*,' he said, his face splitting apart into an amused grin. His eyes were wide with significance. 'He got the biscuits there too – I think she gave them to him from her own pantry.'

Valerie was touched. As she watched Henri get to work on washing the glass of the front door, his hands wringing a rag full of the soapy water, she picked up the tea her grandfather had made, and though it was absolutely terrible – weak, and devoid of sugar – she enjoyed every last sip.

As the afternoon wore on, Valerie realised that she wasn't ready to find out how she was conceived, who her father was. She knew that she should just get it over with, go and see Madame Joubert, and put things right between them, but she just couldn't. She sent Henri over with a note, saying that she would need to reschedule.

She was startled when she heard the phone ring. It was Freddy. The line was bad, tinny.

'Haven't got long, love, but I just wanted to hear your voice.'

She grinned. 'Thanks. How's it going there?'

'Honestly?'

'Yes.'

'It's bloody miserable. Can't say much, walls have ears and all of that… but it's bleak here. I spoke to some of the people who got through the wall, their lives…' There was a pause and she could picture him talking a drag of a cigarette, rubbing his eyes. He was always like this when he was on a story – it was all-consuming. 'It's like the world has gone mad, sometimes.'

He was right. The latest news about the Cuban missile crisis was shocking enough. People were coming into the shop with all kinds of fears, some preparing for the end of days, wanting manuals about 'living off the grid' and 'surviving the apocalypse'.

They even had a section for people who were building bomb shelters in their homes.

Some days it was funny, but it wasn't really, not when you stopped to think about it. What if there really was a nuclear war?

'Just be careful, Freddy.'

'Always,' he said, then took another drag of his cigarette. 'Chat later, love, one of the guys has arrived now for an interview – got to run.'

And he was off.

She sighed, put the phone back in the cradle, and picked up the bookshop cat, giving him a hug.

'That boy of yours okay?' asked Dupont. He was coming into the shop with a fillet of fish. It was a Friday and, Cuban missile crisis or not, the man would cook his fish.

She nodded, her face sinking back into its glum lines.

He stared at her for some time, seeming to make up his mind about something. Eventually, he said, 'Would you like to watch a film?'

She looked up. 'A film?'

'There is an old cinema around the corner. They are playing *Gone with the Wind*, again, and I thought if you wanted… we could go?'

He wanted to watch a film with her?

She grinned. 'That sounds great.'

He nodded. '*Bon*.' Giving her a rare smile.

Later that evening they sat on old velvet seats eating popcorn and drinking wine out of short glasses, and watching Scarlett fall in love with Rhett. She laughed more at Dupont's deep rumbling laughter than she did the story, and it was the first time in ages that she had felt that maybe things might just be all right.

After she had got ready for bed, hearing the night-time sounds of Dupont – his clicking ankle as he made his way up the stairs, putting the cat out – she slipped under the sheets and leant her head against the peeling wallpaper. She had to tell him who she really was. She knew that. But then she thought back on the day, a day that had started off badly, with her feeling dispirited and worried about Freddy, the threat of war, the past, and how each time she'd sunk into those black moods, Dupont had been there to cheer her up. She felt tears prick her eyes as she realised just how much she had come to care for him, and how hard it would be if he turned her away now. 'Oh, Amélie,' she whispered, 'maybe you were right – maybe I was just asking for trouble, with this.'

In the morning, Madame Joubert came by, bringing fresh croissants from the bakery and a bouquet of sweet-smelling irises.

When Dupont was occupied making coffee, Madame Joubert turned to her, and Valerie looked down at her feet. 'I know what you are going to say.'

'No, you don't. You know what you think I am going to say – that's different. Come tonight, we can go out for dinner.'

Valerie agreed; this time she knew there was no getting out of it.

She met Madame Joubert at Les Deux Magots, the famous cafe that had once been the haunt of Hemingway, Fitzgerald and a host of other famous writers and artists. She could picture them sitting there, arguing and laughing in the rose-coloured sunshine, writing their masterpieces and falling in love with the city.

But then just as easily, seeing Madame Joubert – her open face sad, her curls looking unusually flat, as she sipped a glass of port waiting for Valerie at the back – she could also picture the cafe twenty years before, under the veil of the Occupation, see how the French had been turned into spectators in their own cities. Watching as the Germans fed themselves on their wine, their food and their way of life.

She took a seat next to Madame Joubert, who smiled at her. 'I'm glad you came, *chérie*. I thought this would be a nice place to come. Touristy, yes, but we mustn't forget what makes Paris Paris, *non*? It's what we fought for, in the end.'

Valerie nodded. When the waiter came past, a young man with a thin smile, slicked-back hair and dark eyes, she ordered a whisky, deciding that for what Madame Joubert was about to tell her, she was going to need something strong to drink.

At first they spoke of the bookshop, and Freddy. Madame Joubert was glad that it had finally worked out for them, though saddened to hear that he was in West Berlin. 'That sounds dangerous,' she said. Valerie nodded. No more dangerous than what Madame

Joubert and M'sieur Dupont had lived through, though – at least they were no longer at war.

Valerie took a sip of her whisky, and they ran out of casual topics and things to fill the silence, to delay what she had come here to learn. She took a deep breath, her chest rising up and down, and blurted out, 'She was raped, yes? My mother?'

Madame Joubert choked on her port, and started to cough. She raised a blue-and-white checked napkin to dab the red juices that ran all along her chin, her eyes watering.

Valerie stared at her for some time, before remembering her manners. 'C-can I get you some water?'

Madame Joubert shook her head. 'It went down the wrong way.' Her voice was raspy and she took a breath, but she stared at Valerie for a long while before she said, at last, 'Your mother wasn't raped.'

'She wasn't?'

Madame Joubert shook her head.

Valerie breathed out in relief; it had been one of her fears. She hadn't realised how much it had been eating at her. But as she sat in the crowded cafe, and realised what the alternative meant – that her mother had *chosen* to sleep with a Nazi – she didn't know if in the end that was somehow worse.

CHAPTER TWENTY

1940

Mattaus Fredericks came home to darkness. The apartment had not a shred of light on, despite the early evening hour.

'Mademoiselle,' he called. For a long while there was nothing, not a sound to stir the dark winter's night, just the wind that rattled the windows and sneaked in through the gaps in the doors. He felt a momentary dart of unease. Had Kroeling come back to finish what he'd started? His mind pictured the worst, and he began to imagine discovering Mireille's body, left broken and abused. But then there was the small sound of her shuffling feet, and she appeared at the door to the kitchen like a mouse.

He breathed a sigh of relief.

'Are you quite all right? Everything is dark.'

She nodded. 'I – I'm quite well, thank you. I have left some dinner for you.'

He could tell that she was far from well. She looked terrified. It made the muscle in his jaw tense. When had that happened? He had only ever wanted to help people, to be a doctor, not the sort of man that young women feared. Not that he could blame her, after all that she had been through in the past forty-eight hours. He could see the bruises Valter Kroeling had left behind on her neck, and along the tops of her arms, purple and painful, no doubt.

He looked away. 'I do not expect you to share your food with me.'

Mireille nodded. 'It's fine. I am used to cooking for two. It's nothing much, just a baked potato and beans. It's on the table.'

As she turned to leave, he stopped her, touching her shoulder lightly, and she gasped in fear. Her blue eyes were like a startled rabbit's.

He raised his palms, his eyes wary. 'Sorry. I wanted to know – why was everything in the dark? I was told also that you did not open the shop today. Why not?'

She hesitated, deciding on whether or not she should tell him about the Frenchman who had lurked outside the shop all day, the one with venom in his eyes every time he looked at her, and when he spat at her feet.

'How did you know that I did not open the shop?'

He sucked his bottom lip for a moment, then looked away. 'I sent someone to look out for you – to keep watch, in case Kroeling comes back. The man will ensure that I get here in time.'

'Th-thank you.'

It was the second occasion in such a short passage of time that she'd found herself taken aback by his kindness.

When he put on the light in the kitchen and asked her if she would join him, she felt that she owed him that at least.

She took a seat opposite him. He poured them both a glass of wine, and then looked at her face for longer than she would have preferred. 'I have some ointment that you can put on that,' he said, pointing to a thin wound above her eye where Kroeling had hit her.

She nodded, and watched him eat. After a while her heart rate began to slow, and she felt, for the first time since Kroeling's attack, something close to calm.

There was something about the ordinary sounds of cutlery on a plate that made life feel, for a moment, normal.

She sipped her wine, and wondered at how it had come to this.

It turned out that the man Mattaus Fredericks had hired to keep watch over her in case Kroeling returned was the oily-haired Frenchman who had spat at her feet. She supposed he came cheap, and she supposed, as well, that this was why the man had sworn at her as he had. Currying favour with the Germans, particularly when you were a woman, was not looked upon in a soft light, especially by those who were hardest hit, like the poor or the old. Mireille wouldn't waste her breath trying to explain that it wasn't by choice; she knew that someone like him would never understand anyway. He was the sort of man who believed, perhaps, that what you wore or how pretty your face was meant that you were in some way 'asking for it'. The truth was it was none of his business: she knew that she was no traitor – which should have been enough for anyone else.

The trouble was that he wasn't the only one who began whispering about her. The neighbours didn't take the news well that a Nazi officer was living alone with an unwed young girl, while her father was in jail.

There were some who started calling her names in the street. '*Putain*, slut,' hissed an old woman who came into the bookshop especially one morning that week. 'Filthy whore,' said a girl who used to go to school with her. Mireille sat shaking in her chair afterwards; even when she'd attempted to explain, her friend hadn't wanted to hear it. But it was different for her – she had three sisters and a mother, unlike Mireille, who was all alone.

The worst of that week was still to come, however, in the form of Valter Kroeling himself. Mireille was dusting the shelves, many of which were now emptier than they'd ever been, the stock old, as few people were buying books apart from the Nazis, when she looked up and her heart started to thud in sudden fear. He was walking towards her, his pale blue eyes gleaming with something like hatred, and triumph.

Mireille's knees turned to jelly, and if she hadn't been holding on to the shelf she would probably have sunk to the floor. She battled to get air into her lungs. The night that he'd come at her was strong in her mind – the pain, the terror – and she felt sure that if no one else were in the shop she would have begun screaming. She looked away, tried to calm her breathing, grateful beyond belief that she wasn't alone this time.

Kroeling strolled inside the shop, a sneer on his face as he took in the changes that she had made to the store in the past few days. To take her mind off her troubles and fears, she had attempted to return the store to its original set-up, apart from a small but thoroughly reviled area where there was still a table piled with the hated pamphlets that the Nazis distributed, telling the Parisians their new rules, the new sets of indignities under which they were forced to live.

As he got closer, she found her courage and squared her shoulders, setting her jaw. If he attacked her this time, in front of her customers, she would go down fighting, even if it killed her or him.

But he stopped just inches from her face. His hands hung loosely at his sides. His eyes glittered with scorn. 'I see your doctor has moved in now, so that's how it is, eh? You were holding out for a captain?' He gave a fake laugh, and Mireille felt nauseated – she could see on the side of his head the bruises from where her father had hit him with the chair. She hoped it still hurt.

She sneered. 'That's right.'

He made a small sound, his tongue between his teeth, like a hiss. Then he shrugged, feigning an air of nonchalance. 'But he's nothing special. Just a lowly doctor – it's not a proper rank. He has no real authority, despite the way he acts.' He came forward and grinned, right in her face. 'If I had known that you ached for someone more powerful, you should have said. I'm due a promotion soon, if that's what matters to you,' he leered, his eyes roaming her body.

'It doesn't, I can assure you. Get out, you have no business here any more,' she hissed.

They were drawing a crowd of spectators and Valter Kroeling seemed to be enjoying that. 'What?' he asked, as a few older women backed away from a small discount section of cheap paperbacks.

Then he turned back to Mireille and laughed in her face. 'I get it now – you don't like being called a whore. You like to be courted first, is that it?' he said, his eyes glittering, licking his sharp, thin teeth with his tongue. 'Shall I buy a little book first, like Herr Doctor, and then you'll let me into your drawers? Is that the price it takes?'

She looked away. 'You're disgusting.'

He pressed his face up to hers. 'No, *you* are. I thought at least you were pure, that you were a proud little French girl, putting up with these nasty Germans,' he snorted, 'but you are just like all these other French whores, parting your legs for the highest bidder.' Then he turned and marched out of the shop, saying over his shoulder, 'And you'd better put out more pamphlets – I'll be back tomorrow to check. It's the only reason we've still let you keep this shop.'

Somehow she managed not to throw something at the back of his head.

Later that night, bone tired from lying awake tossing and turning and worrying about Kroeling's threat, she heard a noise coming from the back of the apartment by the stairs. It sounded like scratching.

She hurried down the stairs, pressing her ear to the door, frowning as she heard what sounded like low sobbing.

The doctor hadn't come home yet, but sometimes he was late from the hospital.

She felt safer when he was there. She kept all the doors locked just in case. Her hands shook. What if it was Valter Kroeling again? What if he knocked down the door? It was past midnight; she doubted that the man Mattaus Fredericks had paid to look out for her hung on past then, not when he could spend the money on drink.

Then she heard a faint voice call, from the other side of the door, 'Mireille.'

'Clotilde?' she whispered.

There was a faint 'It's me' on the other side, and Mireille scrabbled to open the door, her heart lifting. She'd been worried about Clotilde, whom she hadn't seen for days, and was relieved that she was finally home now, at last – only to catch her breath as she found her friend leaning against the opposite wall, her clothes torn and filthy, with dried blood in her hair, and all down her face.

Mireille gasped, then dragged her inside. 'Are you hurt? What happened? Oh, Clotilde.'

Clotilde looked at her with her deep, dark eyes. 'I got away.'

'What do you mean?' Mireille's heart started to thud – was no one she loved safe?

'I was followed. I should have listened to you – it's true, since that Nazi Valter Kroeling started haunting you, we've been watched. One of his men caught me passing information in the park about the movements of the officers, their schedules – there was a plan to attack.'

Mireille's knees turned weak. How deep had her friend got?

'He tried to take me. But I fought him off. You know the penalty,' she said, her voice breaking.

Mireille closed her eyes. It was death by firing squad.

Clotilde began to shake and sob.

'Oh, my dear,' said Mireille, pulling her friend into a hug and leading her to a chair. The first thing she needed to do was to assess the damage. Then they could figure out what to do. If there was somewhere she could hide Clotilde, perhaps… She got a clean washcloth out of the cupboard, along with some iodine. She wrung the cloth out under the tap, and tended her friend's wounds, getting up afterwards to fetch her father's whisky and pour them each a large glass.

'I heard about your father – that he was arrested. Is it true?' asked Clotilde. Her large eyes were full of pity.

While they drank, Mireille told her about what had happened – how badly things had gone wrong with Valter Kroeling, and how her father was now in prison.

Clotilde closed her eyes. 'I should have been here!'

'It would have made no difference.'

Clotilde nodded. 'Maybe.' She clutched her head. Then she stood up after a moment. 'I must go. That man has my name – it is only a matter of time before he comes here, and I have heard that they deal swiftly with resisters for what I have done, beating up that officer… I just needed to see you, even if it's only to say goodbye.' Her voice broke.

Mireille stood up fast, too. 'No, don't leave! Where will you go, Clotilde? Let's talk about this – there must be somewhere I can hide you. If you run, they'll find you. You're all I have left! I can't let anything happen to you.'

A voice behind them made them jump. 'She can stay here, for now.'

Mireille turned slowly, ashen, and saw at the bottom of the stairs leading into the bookshop Mattaus. How long had he been standing there?

He came into the room, and walked straight to Clotilde, who recoiled, looking from him to Mireille in fear. Mireille didn't know how to begin explaining.

'I – thought it best to sleep downstairs, in the storeroom,' he said, by way of explanation.

Had he been here this whole time? She frowned.

'That looks painful,' he said, looking at Clotilde. 'May I?' He came forward to peer at her face. Clotilde jumped at his touch.

'He – he's a doctor,' said Mireille, trying and failing to slow her beating heart. Clotilde looked as if she were ready to bolt, and flinched when Mattaus laid his fingers along her skull, testing the flesh.

'It is not cracked. Just bruised, I think. You will need stitches, though, above that eye. I will do it. I have something for the pain, from my bag downstairs… give me a moment.'

As he left, Clotilde looked at Mireille, and hissed, quickly, 'What is he doing here? Should I run? Can he be trusted?'

As quickly as she dared, she told her friend of the arrangement.

'He's here because your father asked him to look out for you? *Dupont*?'

Mireille nodded. 'Yes.'

Clotilde shook her head. 'And instead of encroaching on your flat, your space – he's been sleeping in the storeroom?'

'It seems like it. Yes.'

After a beat Clotilde shook her head. 'I didn't know there were ones like him.'

Mireille nodded. She hadn't either. But still…

'I don't know that we *can* trust him, Clotilde, however nice he seems.'

There was a noise from behind, and Mattaus came back into the room. If he had heard Mireille's words, his face betrayed no sign of it. Mireille closed her eyes, her cheeks flooding with colour.

He didn't say anything as he opened his bag and prepared the stitches. He looked at the open whisky bottle, and nodded at Mireille to pour another. 'I think that will help more than this,' he said of the small bottle of pain medicine he took out.

When he'd finished, he seemed to have been gearing himself up for something, because he took a deep breath and said, 'You can, you know,' to Mireille.

'What?' she asked.

He put his supplies back into his large leather bag and closed it with a dull click. 'Trust me. I will not betray you. Either of you.'

They blinked. Mireille's heart started to pound again.

'But there is something I need to tell you,' he said, turning to Clotilde now. 'There have been talks of rounding up people like you, people of your faith. It has for the moment been rejected but I am not sure for how long. I fear that is the way it will go, soon. If you can get out of the city, that would be wise, and if I can help you to do that, I will.'

'Why?' said Mireille later, after she had helped her friend to bed, and she'd come downstairs to find that this whole time he had been sleeping in the small stock room, on an old couch that was far too small for him, covered in cat hair.

'I thought you might be more comfortable if I was not in the apartment – I saw that you were not sleeping.'

She frowned, shook her head. 'Thank you, but no, I did not mean that – though it is fine, you are welcome to sleep upstairs. This can't be comfortable, and after all it is you who are helping me – the least you should have is a good night's rest from the arrangement.'

'I am fine, believe me. I'm a doctor, used to sleeping where and when I can.'

She nodded, bit her lip, and asked her question again. 'What I wanted to ask was why should we trust you – why would you risk all of this for us?'

He looked down at his feet. 'Isn't it obvious?'

She frowned. 'Not to me.'

He smiled for the first time, and she noticed how handsome he really was, how under normal circumstances she would have enjoyed looking at a face like his, with his cropped dark blond hair, defined cheekbones, tanned skin and bright green eyes.

'Well, it should be. I have done that stupid thing that I was warned against. Fallen for the enemy.'

She took a step back, her heart starting to pound.

'Mireille,' he said. It was the first time he hadn't called her Mademoiselle. 'I don't expect anything from you, or for you to feel the same. This is about me, or the man I used to be, before my country went mad – the world, really – and when I'm with you I think maybe I could be that man again, some day…'

She sat on the edge of his couch. 'What man is that?' she asked quietly.

'Just a doctor, and some day perhaps a husband, a father.'

'Not a soldier? A *Nazi*?' She couldn't help the venom that came with that last word, as much as she tried.

He shook his head, his eyes growing dark. 'No, that was never part of the plan. I was conscripted. I admit that for a while I did believe in some of the things the people who followed Hitler said.'

At Mireille's deepening frown, he tried to explain. 'Germany was a hard place growing up. We were poor, suffering a great depression. Everything the country made went to paying off reparations for a war we never started. People were starving and suffering, and then *he* came, and things got better for a time. Until they got a lot worse, until nothing made sense any more. And suddenly my friends, people who I once debated with about politics and religion and our country, had suddenly become fanatics, not able to see sense. They were brainwashed, and if you spoke out, it was jail or execution. I never wanted *this*, trust me.'

He looked so sad and lost that Mireille felt that suddenly she could truly see the man behind the uniform. She'd been so terrified of having him there. She kept waiting for him to turn into the monster she was sure was lurking behind his pleasant mask. She frowned, then, with shaking fingers, she touched his shoulder. She hadn't ever willingly touched him before, and though it was a small gesture, it was one that would change everything.

He reached out and squeezed her hand, and she left hers in his. For the first time in months she didn't want to be anywhere but where she was, sitting right next to him. Having him look at her the way he did, and having, for just a moment, the feeling that maybe the world might make sense again one day.

CHAPTER TWENTY-ONE

It took a week, with Clotilde hiding in the apartment, for Mattaus to get the false identity papers for her to leave the country.

Already several officials had come to check if Clotilde had come back to the apartment. Each time, thankfully, Mattaus had been on hand to answer their questions, and to show them around – proving that that she wasn't. He didn't show them everything, of course. Like where they had actually hidden her, which was in the attic. There was a moment when one of the men looked up at the ceiling as if thinking about it, but when he saw Mattaus looking at him with a raised brow, he nodded, then left.

They had all breathed a sigh of relief after that.

'These papers will help you to leave, via Spain. There is a man who will help you to cross the border.'

They'd dyed Clotilde's hair blonde the night before, and she would be leaving with the doctor in one of Mireille's dresses. It showed how thin her friend had become that it fitted her, despite the difference in their height. It broke Mireille's heart seeing her so reduced.

The doctor and Clotilde went over the plan once again as Mireille watched Clotilde pack her bag, tears streaming down her cheeks. When would she see her friend again?

'You will let me know, somehow, that you are safe?' she asked for the third time that morning, and Clotilde nodded, pressed her close to her chest.

'I will, I promise.' Then she blew out her cheeks, and said, 'I think he might be one of the good ones.'

Mireille nodded, then gave her one last squeeze as Mattaus told her to hurry: the car was waiting outside.

When Clotilde was at the stairs, Mattaus turned back to Mireille. 'I will go with her as far as Lyon, then come back later tonight, from the hospital. It will take some time before we get word that she has crossed the border – you must be strong.'

She nodded, and when he reached out to squeeze her hand, she gave him one in response.

Worry consumed Mireille's days. Worry about her father and for her friend. Every day she had been turned away by the prison – no one would let her see her father. But after a time one of the younger guards took pity on her and gave her an update. He was thin, and had a scar on the side of his lip, but his eyes were kind.

'You don't need to come every day,' he said. 'We are not mistreating him.'

She nodded. There was something about him that made her believe that what he said was true.

Mireille tried to make it enough that he wasn't being abused, but she still continued to visit, still continued to worry. There were other fears she had for him – disease, starvation, loneliness… there was only one of those she might be able to help prevent.

'Can you give him this?' she asked the guard, passing him a boiled turnip wrapped in a cloth. 'I have heard that there is not enough food here.'

'There is not enough food anywhere,' he said. They stared at each other for some time, then eventually he gave a slight nod.

'Can I bring some more for him?'

The guard didn't say anything for a while, and Mireille worried that she'd gone too far, that he would throw the vegetable in her face, but he sighed, and nodded. Perhaps he hoped that somewhere, somehow, someone was treating his own father well. 'Come this time again tomorrow.'

It took three days for her to get word that Clotilde had entered Spain and was safe. For the first time in days, Mireille felt that she could breathe. In the time since her friend had fled, she had been walking around in a daze, barely seeing Mattaus's face, just drawing comfort from his continued presence, and his frequent assurances that no news at this stage was good news.

When Mattaus came home that night, after she had got the news, she ate dinner with him, and before she got up to leave the table, she touched his hair and kissed his forehead. His hand reached out for hers. His green eyes were intense, dark, and she felt her stomach flip. When he stood up to kiss her properly, her heart began to thud. She closed her eyes as his lips met hers, and sank into his kiss.

CHAPTER TWENTY-TWO

1941

It was spring when her father was finally released and he came home weak and half starved despite the food she had managed to sneak in. He'd given most of it away to another prisoner who had begun coughing up blood.

He'd grown ever more angry as a result of his time in jail, his resentment towards the Germans a festering wound that would not heal.

Despite the fact that he'd asked Mattaus to stay with his daughter, he didn't like it at all, seething with unspent rage that the doctor didn't move out now that he was back. He wanted his home, his privacy, a refuge away from them, but he felt doomed never to get it.

Mireille cared for her father as best she could, trying to temper his anger and get him to eat, but his stomach was poor, and could only take so much after so many months of poor nutrition.

As they moved into the summer of 1941, rationing had become ever more onerous. Turnips had become a key staple of their daily diet, despite the small extras the doctor brought home, which had become less and less as the city needed more, and the farms stopped producing. All the food was needed for the soldiers.

'I am home now – why doesn't he leave?' complained Vincent for the third time that week, listening to the movements downstairs as the doctor got ready for bed.

'You know why, Papa,' Mireille said. 'As long as he's here, Valter Kroeling is not.'

Her father nodded and lit one of the cigarettes that came from the doctor's supply. 'I suppose we are to be grateful for that.'

'Yes.'

He rubbed his eyes. He would be grateful only when this was over, when they had left his city, and his home.

Mireille waited for her father to fall asleep before she slipped downstairs and crept into the storeroom where Mattaus was still sleeping – he'd refused to encroach further on their apartment. Mireille had cleared it up as much as possible, so at least it was more comfortable.

Mattaus looked up at the sound of the creaking door, then sat up quickly when he saw it was Mireille. He was only in a pair of white boxers.

Mireille closed the door, and leant against it. She was wearing her best negligee, from before the war. It was the only one she had now.

She swallowed. Her breathing quickened.

'Mireille?'

She stared at him, at his body. He was a big man. Tall, fit and muscular. The skin on his arms, neck and face was tanned.

She was suddenly very nervous. This had all seemed like such a good idea, until it actually came down to it. She couldn't sleep, and the more Papa had complained about Mattaus, the more she'd realised just how angry she was becoming at what he said, and how she'd come to care for this man who had risked everything for her, including helping her friend to escape the country.

His teeth were even and white. Her stomach flipped at how handsome he was, especially when he smiled.

'Hello,' he said softly. 'I've been thinking about things.'

'What things?' she asked, taking a step closer in her bare feet. She sat down on the edge of the old sofa, aware of how thin the negligee was, how much of herself was exposed. There was very little room; most of it was taken up by him. His legs were warm against hers.

He looked at her, then shook his head, laughter lines showing around his bright green eyes as he said simply, 'You.'

She bit her lip. 'And what do you think about when you think of me?'

'Everything.'

He pulled her towards him and kissed her, and soon she was beneath him and his hands and lips were everywhere, trailing kisses along her neck, her shoulders, her breasts. She had to bite her lip to stop herself from moaning out, till they reached even further, parting her thighs. His lips caused shivers as he whispered in her ear, 'Are you sure you want to do this?'

She nodded. Right then he was the only thing in her life she was sure of.

CHAPTER TWENTY-THREE

She found out that she was pregnant eight weeks later, when she could no longer fit into her dress, despite the fact that they were surviving on turnips and the occasional bit of meat.

Mattaus examined her, and when he confirmed it, she spent the rest of the evening sobbing.

They called women like her traitors and whores. They spat at the ones who had children by German officers: people kicked them, and pinched, and they promised that when this war finally came to an end, women like her would be the first ones they killed.

It didn't matter that she had fallen for Mattaus, that he was different, that he hadn't wanted this war. No one would ever believe her. But what would happen to her baby? How would it be treated – as a pariah? Raised to hate itself for nothing it had done wrong? She'd seen how women in the street eyed the babies of Nazi soldiers, when they were taken out by their fathers, as if they would throw them under a bus.

Mattaus rocked her against his chest, and made soothing noises. For Mattaus this was the best thing that had happened to him since Mireille had first climbed into his bed – he was going to be a father, and, if she let him, a husband. For Mireille it was another example of how something that should have been a happy, almost everyday moment, had become tainted and reshaped due to the infernal war.

They got married in secret. In a small church, with a priest they paid in food.

The holy man didn't hide his disdain, but it didn't matter to Mattaus or Mireille what he thought. They knew what they had, but she was terrified of how she would tell her father.

Mattaus suggested that they break the news to him that night and she agreed.

Her father sank into a chair at the news, his face seeming to age in an instant. He looked tired, and thin, and old. Just the day before he had lost several teeth which had become rotten from his time in jail. But this seemed the hardest news to bear even so.

His eyes were shocked. 'Pregnant by a Nazi.'

Mireille closed her eyes. 'Papa, I'm sorry.'

Dupont shook his head. 'No. Don't.' His face was angry, twisted in pain. She had never seen him look so defeated, so broken as he did now. She felt her stomach drop – she hated that she had caused it.

Tears leaked down her cheeks. 'I tried not to fall for him,' she said, her voice small.

Her father closed his eyes. After a while he shook his head and said, 'I told him to stay – it is my fault. You were left alone with him, what else did I think would happen?'

'No, Papa, that was a good decision, he is a good man.'

Dupont grunted.

Mattaus was silent, didn't flinch when her father insulted him. 'I will look after your daughter, I promise. I love her.'

Dupont didn't say anything. Just sat and shook his head, his face full of pain as he repeated, 'Pregnant.'

CHAPTER TWENTY-FOUR

1962

'So that was why he sent me away,' breathed Valerie. The cafe had grown quiet – they were two of the last to leave – yet still they sat, still they drank, as Madame Joubert, her mother's oldest, dearest friend, told her everything her grandfather had tried desperately for her never to know. Because she owed it to her friend, and the love that had saved her own life.

'Yes.'

'Dupont blamed himself?'

'Yes. I think he wanted to like Mattaus, and before he went to prison, he might have, but after spending several months in a Nazi-run jail, he came out hating them all even more than before. But he was not alone; a lot of them were like that. It was understandable – trust me, as a Jewish woman, I am the first to shout out my hatred of the Nazis, but some took it too far. Especially when it came to the children who had German fathers. People saw them as something that needed to be brought as much pain as they had endured. These children were ridiculed, stigmatised and ostracised. Even to this day. There are some who were never accepted by the rest of their families, who grew up with deep psychological scars as a result. Dupont is many things, but he loved his daughter, and he loved you – and when she died, he made the decision, however hard it must have been, to send you away so that you wouldn't have to endure the prejudice. I think it's what he wished he could have had the courage to do with Mireille – to send her to the countryside when the Germans invaded. I think with you he thought he would have a second chance to get it right, even if it broke his heart.'

When Valerie went home that night she thought of all that Madame Joubert had told her. She tried to make sense of her own prejudices, her own beliefs, and to match these somehow against those of her mother's, and indeed her father's. Could she understand how a woman in her mother's situation would have fallen for a man like Mattaus Fredericks? Yes, was the honest answer. Like her mother, loyalty was a key part of her heart, her make-up, and she could well understand how, after risking his own life to save her friend's, she could also have fallen for him. The revelation brought with it something new to the discovery of who her father was – it eased the wellspring of shame that had curled itself tight around her chest at finding out that he had been a Nazi soldier. She knew, however, that she couldn't know all that was in his heart. She couldn't be sure that on every score he was a good man, as Madame Joubert had told her there had been a time that he had believed in what the party stood for. But she supposed it was the person who came through in the end that mattered to her most – the kind of person who did what was right no matter the cost, even if that meant turning traitor to his country and its rules. In many ways he was, she realised, the person she needed most to understand.

Rain battered the window as she slipped inside the bedcovers – sleep would be a long time in coming that night, once again.

In the morning she found that Dupont had made her another cup of tea, and she smiled as she looked down at it. *At some point,* she thought, *I am really going to have to teach him how to make the stuff properly.*

He caught her looking at him a few times that morning as she thought of him, and the decision he'd made to send her away. She was beginning to understand, she realised, how he would have believed it was the right decision. Part of her felt something then that she hadn't expected to feel for him all those months ago when she first arrived at the bookshop. It was pity.

But there was still a part of her that couldn't believe what Madame Joubert had said… that he'd loved her. Perhaps he had in his own way, but wasn't it also likely that he wanted to send her somewhere far away, so that he could be spared the pain of looking at her, of always being reminded of where she'd come from?

When she and Madame Joubert had left Les Deux Magots the night before, they had walked along the Seine, each in their own way not ready to leave just yet. Night had fallen and they could hear the soft call of birdsong, and the thrum of a guitar coming from one of the riverboats.

The lights along the riverbank cast golden ribbons along the water, and they reflected in Valerie's green eyes as she turned to Madame Joubert, a frown between them. They were speaking about the day Valerie had been taken out of Paris, and Madame Joubert had shaken her head, her red curls glowing chestnut in the night air. 'It was just after the war ended,' insisted the older woman as Valerie frowned, protesting, 'But I remember it *during* the war. I'm sure I do. The way we ran… the taste of our fear. Amélie picked me up, and on one of the streets there were all these soldiers. Amélie was afraid of them, I could tell. It had to still be during the war, when she came to take me with her.'

Madame Joubert snuggled into her thick woollen scarf as she sighed. 'No. It was after the war – the soldiers you saw were our own. She feared for you because of them. It was a panicky time, and it wasn't clear what was going to happen to the children of the people they had assembled for what was called "the purge". The city wanted to rid itself of every last reminder of the Occupation. To punish all those people who had collaborated with the Germans – the women who had slept with them, the men who had done business with them. The hunger for retribution against these people who, in the hearts and minds of many of the Parisians who had to suffer while some of their own seemed to benefit, was great. Dupont worried what this might mean for you – would these children be rounded up and taken away to some camp? Sent to an orphanage? Even if you weren't taken away, the other reality that was sure to befall you growing up here was that you would never be seen as one of us, that you would always be treated as an outsider...'

Madame Joubert told her then the story of a young boy she had heard of who had killed himself the year he turned thirteen. His father had been German, and he was teased mercilessly every day, until one day he just couldn't bear it any more and he threw himself off a bridge. Another young man went looking for his German family after the treatment he'd suffered as the child of one of these unfortunate matches. 'I don't know what it's like on the other side – if the children of the allies were treated any better in Germany. If I have learnt anything about human nature during this time, I suspect not. But I can tell you that your grandfather believed that the war you had to face would be after the Occupation, and on the streets of Paris, as you tried and failed to justify your existence to people who were deeply wounded and angry that such a thing had ever been allowed to occur. That's why he sent you to live with Amélie. He wanted to spare you the pain of ever feeling that you didn't belong...'

'Except that there were times I felt that way anyway. I always knew that I didn't fit. That there was something that didn't add up.'

Madame Joubert nodded. 'I know.'

Valerie looked at Madame Joubert, and shook her head. 'But it's true – I was spared that hatred, that suffering. I felt like an outsider sometimes, but it wasn't due to anyone's cruelty. I've had a good life, filled with love, kindness, friendship.'

Madame Joubert's shoulders started to shake at this, and Valerie realised that Dupont wasn't the only one who would have been seeking absolution for the decision to send her to be raised by Amélie. She touched Madame Joubert's shoulder.

'I can see that I wouldn't have had that here – it would have been a wedge between me and the world.'

Growing up, Amélie had been aunt and mother to her. She'd known love and kindness. She'd never been made to feel the way some of the other children like her had no doubt been made to feel.

Valerie suspected that her grandfather's decision to give her away, and the reasons behind it, would take a lifetime to process. It was easy to say now, when one wasn't at war and not subjected to its power to test you on every level, to put your will for survival above your ideals, what you would have done.

They had drifted off towards the block of apartments on the Rue des Oiseaux after midnight. The older woman's arm was around her shoulders, and when they had said goodnight, Valerie felt for just a moment that she could see that girl, the woman who had been part of the resistance, fierce and loyal to a fault, a young Clotilde, as she slipped up the stairs to her apartment on the right.

CHAPTER TWENTY-FIVE

The phone rang in the bookshop, and Valerie answered: 'Gribouiller.'

In the background Dupont shouted, looking up from the accounts, a gnarled, cigarette-stained finger stabbing a page full of figures, a large calculator at his side, 'If that is Timothe Babin, tell him from me that he is shameless to try to call you, and get you to do it in secret. I won't do it. I will *not* order any more of that blasted Fleming's books. I don't care if there is to be a new film. Or if it will star that Scotsman. That, in my opinion, only makes it *worse*.'

'Is that your grandfather screaming in the background?' came Freddy's voice.

Valerie grinned. She shoved a pencil behind her ear, and asked, 'Define screaming?'

The line crackled slightly. 'Um, they can hear it all the way in East Berlin, and they've said they've got enough problems, so they've asked me to tell him to turn it down.'

Valerie laughed. 'What can I do for you, Mr Lea-Sparrow?'

'We-ll…' Which resulted in a rather dirty few minutes, and Valerie turning rather pink in her chair.

'Fred-*dy*, people could be listening. When are you coming home?'

'It might be sooner than you think…'

'Really? How soon?' she exclaimed, her slumped shoulders straightening.

'Very.'

'What does that mean?'

'Look up.'

She frowned, then looked up and yelped in glee. There he was. She made a mental note to check the payphone outside every time Freddy called from now on.

He laughed, and said into the mouthpiece, 'I don't think this will ever get old…'

But she didn't hear him – she was already running across the street, dodging a passing car, which honked its hooter at her, a flurry of curse words following her as she ran into his arms.

When she raced back inside the shop a few minutes later to ask if she could take her lunch early, breathless and happy, her long blonde hair streaming behind her, Dupont just snorted and sent her off with the words: 'Thank God, now at least I can stop making that horrible muck to get you to cheer up. Go – go.'

She left with a chuckle, taking her jacket with her, and together she and Freddy set off arm in arm for his apartment. They bought a bottle of wine on the way, as well as some fresh baguettes from the bakery on the corner, and some cheese that smelt so bad in his tiny bar fridge that later they would regret it, and had a picnic in bed after a more intimate greeting altogether.

'I think I have corrupted you,' Freddy said, smiling with one side of his face.

She laughed, her green eyes alight. 'Amélie said that when we were just kids. I remember it exactly – it was, "that boy will bring you no end of trouble". She was right, too. Lots of *trouble*.' She giggled.

He grinned and shrugged a bare shoulder.

As they picked their way through their small feast, Valerie popping a small chunk of baguette in her mouth and chewing, she told him what Madame Joubert had revealed to her about her mother.

Freddy leant his dark tousled head against the headboard and took a drag of the cigarette he'd lit. He was unshaven, and the five o'clock stubble made him look older. 'So they fell in love?' he said. 'Well, it's understandable, I suppose, when you're put through something like that – the fear she had with that officer stalking her, and this other man coming to her defence, the way he kept trying to help her… who wouldn't, really?'

It was one of the things she'd come to love most about him, she realised: how fair he was. How he never saw things in black or white.

'Yeah,' she said. 'I was having a hard time with it – with her falling for him – even though I understand why it happened, even though he did seem to be good…' She pulled a face. 'I can't help but wish that she hadn't.'

He looked at her. 'But then you wouldn't be here, Val. Nope, sorry, but I'm kind of grateful that she fell into his bed. Nazi or not.'

She laughed. She wished she could see it the way he did, so without judgement. She knew it was something she would need to process, work her way through. Even she had her own prejudices, the result of the aftermath of the war, and this would mean unpicking these from the person who was her father, the man who had once been a Nazi, and the shame of knowing that part of her history, as a result of all that she'd learnt, was now on the 'wrong' side – had been responsible for some of the worst acts of humanity, however much of a good man her father seemed.

CHAPTER TWENTY-SIX

1963

Valerie found the diary by accident not long into the new year. She'd been thumbing through Dupont's somewhat sticky collection of cookbooks on the kitchen shelf, when she saw a leather tip poking out between a book about Provençal dinners and another on French family classics. She pulled it out, sensing it misplacement, only to open the small leather-bound book and find herself staring at her mother's neat, slanted handwriting. Her breath caught in her throat. There, recorded in her mother's own hand, were her first moments in this world.

The day she arrived: *12 March 1942*. Her weight: *3.5 kilograms*.

But it was the first line that jumped out at her, making her close the book, her heart jackhammering in her chest.

Valerie Fredericks.

She put a hand on her chest, as she gasped in realisation. Her surname was *German*.

That afternoon, while she tidied up the shelves, her mind kept jolting at the new discovery, like a record that kept skipping. Fredericks. *My surname is Fredericks.* Her fingers shook, and she craved the feel of a cigarette between them, the release that it gave as she sucked the toxins deep into her lungs, drowning out the weight of all her thoughts.

Why had the discovery sent her reeling? she wondered. She had known that her mother had married him – wouldn't it make sense that she had his surname? It did, but it had still come as a shock, just another one of those things she hadn't known about who she was. Why couldn't her aunt and uncle – Dupont, even – have just told her when she was little? Even if she could understand the decision to have her raised elsewhere, why did so much of her past need to be kept a secret from her?

Later that night, she went to Madame Joubert's apartment. The older woman opened the door wearing a patterned blue kimono, her bright red curls striking against the fabric, a small frown between her eyes at having a visitor so late at night – but it cleared when she saw it was Valerie. '*Chérie*?'

Valerie showed her the diary. 'I found this. It belonged to my mother. Can I come in?'

Madame Joubert's eyes widened. 'Of course, *chérie*. Are you all right?'

'I'm not sure,' said Valerie honestly.

Light was coming from a small lamp in the corner of the living room. Valerie was ushered to a seat on the green velvet sofa and offered a drink.

'Wine, please.'

Madame Joubert poured her a glass, and came to take a seat next to her.

'May I?' she said, indicating the book.

Valerie nodded, watching as she opened the leather-bound book, her fingers pausing as she touched the pages. A hand fluttered to her heart. 'It's about you,' she breathed.

Valerie nodded. Tears pricked her eyes as she cleared her throat, trying to clear the sudden swell of emotion too.

'I just – wanted to show someone, someone who would understand.'

Madame Joubert nodded. She flipped through the pages, and Valerie looked on as she did. She hadn't been able to keep going by herself. She caught her breath as she saw another person's handwriting, messier, a man's, she guessed, and she realised with a jolt that it must have been her father's.

'It's like a small journal,' she breathed. With tiny entries and snapshots into their lives. Written when Mireille, no doubt, never imagined that one day it would be found like this.

Together they read a passage that brought instant tears to both their eyes.

> *There are five cries that I have identified so far. The midwife, Lisette, said that one day I would know them all. But there is one that is just for me, for her mother. It is when I leave the room, and it is the one that breaks my heart the most.*

Valerie took a sip of wine, a finger coming up to wipe away the wetness by her eyes that just kept coming. She realised then what had been disturbing her the most about the discovery of the baby book, more so than the name 'Fredericks': it was her mother's story, in her own words. It made it real, somehow, more real than anything she'd heard before.

Madame Joubert read out another passage, smiling through her own misty eyes.

> *I have been blessed with an easy baby. While I have no sphere of reference to judge, I know, I feel certain that in this I have been luckier than most. Valerie sleeps through the night. I have to confess to waking her up sometimes just because I have missed her. M does not approve.*

Madame Joubert topped up their glasses. Then she nodded. 'I have something I also want to share with you.'

She went across the room to a handsome antique writing desk with clawed feet, the wood polished and shining in the low amber light. She unlocked the desk with a key that had turned green with age. Inside was a stack of letters.

'Your mother wrote to me, while I was in Spain. She couldn't send them, of course, but she wrote to me anyway.'

She sniffed, her nose red. 'We found them later, beneath the mattress in her room, after…' She let out a small breath.

After she died, Valerie realised. Her fingers shook as she took the small stack from Madame Joubert. They were bound together with florist's string.

Madame Joubert hesitated. 'I – I am glad that you found that book first,' she said, indicating the leather-bound diary. 'It shows that there was a moment before the fear and the worry when they were happy, and almost like any other normal parents. These show' – she made a small noise in the back of her throat to clear it – 'some of her initial tensions. I wondered all this week if I should share it with you, in case you got the wrong idea, judged her perhaps too harshly… she was very worried about the pregnancy at first, and it made things at home very tense.'

Valerie frowned as she looked down at the stack of letters, a small curl of anxiety entering her heart.

Later that night, listening to the sound of Dupont's snores, she opened the first of the letters. She noted the scrawl of her mother's handwriting, how the neat, slanted hand seemed rushed, how the letters flew, some half formed: a sign of her fears and doubts, Valerie realised.

My Dearest Clotilde,

The baby is beginning to grow. Mattaus says it is healthy, despite our limited diet. It grows strong despite it. I should be happy, but I am not. All I feel is fear. It consumes me night and day. Two weeks ago, a pregnant woman who was rumoured to have shared a bed with a German officer was pushed into the street by an angry mob after the news broke about those students who were arrested for going on a protest march. She fell, and someone kicked her. The baby was stillborn. Papa said that was a blessing in disguise for the child. I couldn't believe that he would think that, let alone say it. I was so angry with him. But I have to confess that it would be easier if I hadn't fallen pregnant. It's the child I worry most about… what will happen when it is born, what if we are not there to protect it and an angry mob turns on it? I can't sleep at night with these thoughts running through my head.

Papa has suggested that I go to the countryside for the birth – to a nunnery in Haute-Provence. But the truth is, why would they help a Nazi's wife? Besides, Mattaus would be devastated. He has a vision of us just living a normal life, and I'm trying so hard to believe it could be possible. That this horrible war could come to an end soon…

Perhaps it will. Sometimes when I can't sleep, I think of you in Spain and it brings me comfort. I imagine you in the countryside, somewhere warm, tasting olives, and that one day I will come too. I hope you are well, and that you have put on some of the weight you lost. I think of you so often – I wish there was a way I could actually send this to you, hear your voice. I miss you every day. I found myself staring too hard the other day at a woman with red hair and lips. I didn't even know how to explain why I was crying. But she was kind all the same when she offered me

her handkerchief. I wonder if she would be so kind if she knew my secret… and when I start to show.
M.

Despite the shock of her mother's words, Valerie kept on reading, discovering that in some ways her mother's fears were proven true. As time went on, according to one letter, and Mireille began to show, some of their regular customers stopped coming to the bookshop. Worse was how bitter Dupont had become at the whole scenario.

He just can't accept it. I can see him trying to like Mattaus every day, trying to put aside his doubts, and then every evening having them return like a weight he carries with him, like Atlas. He told me that it was bad enough that I had slept with M, but marrying the man was something he just couldn't understand… I told him that M didn't want his child to grow up a bastard, and he said, 'Won't it be bad enough that the father is a Nazi?' I spent all night crying at that, Clotilde. It's just not who M is… not really…

Valerie closed her eyes. Her grandfather's fears were exactly what she herself had thought when she'd found out. She felt for her mother, trying so hard to convince her father that Mattaus was a good man. That he wasn't like the others.

If he could just get to know him I think he'd understand, he'd see.

Valerie wondered if Mireille had written to Clotilde because she knew that her friend would understand – that of all of them, Mattaus had risked everything, turned traitor, for her. For that, at least, he deserved her love, her trust.

As dawn crested the horizon, and Valerie worked her way through half of the letters, she found that as time passed, her mother's fears began to subside somewhat as her and Mattaus's excitement at having a baby started to take root.

M brought home a gem squash from the market today. It's been weeks since we had anything so exotic – it's usually turnips for our dinner and if we're lucky the occasional potato. M says that's the size of the baby now. He paid a ridiculous sum for the vegetable. I didn't allow anyone to eat it for three days, while I stared at it like an idiot and it turned wrinkly. How you would have laughed at me as I cried when they boiled it for dinner!

Valerie found that it was around this time that Mireille had got the baby book.

I want to keep a record of everything. Men don't really remember this kind of thing. And Maman didn't keep a diary so I don't know how she felt, becoming a mother for the first time. I wish she were here now… she'd know what to say… M has been wonderful throughout, making me put aside my fears. There's so much wonder in his eyes at the thought of being a father. He keeps bringing home little things. Pink things – you can see he wants a girl. I hope it won't break his heart if it's a boy…

It was like stepping back in time, and experiencing it with her. When Mireille wrote of the new clothing rations, Valerie felt she could picture her frustration at not having anything that fitted while being heavily pregnant.

I've had to resort to making these shapeless maternity smocks, as Papa calls them. They look like patchwork quilts – you know how miserably I failed at sewing. I didn't have your skills. I can imagine you, Clotilde, with a cigarette between your red lips whipping up some creation that could rival Madame Chanel's. I, on the other hand, have created two lopsided tents out of my old dresses, and I alternate these two sad garments day in and day out, because when I am no longer pregnant, that's it – I won't be able to buy more clothes. But it's all workable really, apart from the shoes… my ankles are the size of melons and the only things that fit are a pair of house slippers. You wouldn't think I'd get so big on such a limited diet… but there you go. The baby is the size of a marrow now. Sadly M couldn't secure one for our dinner…

In the morning, bleary eyed from lack of sleep, Valerie made herself a strong cup of coffee and read the last of the letters.

The dark liquid missed her lips as she read of the first confrontation her mother had with Valter Kroeling. She quickly got up to get a dishcloth, sponging the paper where the amber liquid had left its stain, as if to highlight the darkness that lay there.

I was at the market when I ran into Kroeling. I've been going to the one in Montmartre… I go there, I confess, because no one knows me there. There's less chance of someone I know coming up to me and asking questions about the baby… and the father. I had got the week's groceries – there's so little now with the rations, hardly any meat. We eat our weight in turnips. Anyway, when I turned away with my string bag, I saw across the street – Kroeling. My legs started to shake, and I grew faint, turning quickly, hoping to hurry away before he saw me, but it was too late. Before I knew it, the vile man was before me, spinning me around, staring at my tent dress in disbelief, his eyes full of hate. 'You're pregnant.'

I tried to wrench my arm away from his, but he was strong, twisting it, enjoying my pain as I pleaded for him to let me go. He had that same look on his face as that time he came at me… and I felt so much fear, but he used his words this time, instead of hitting me. His face twisted in a mixture of lust and pure vile hatred as his gaze raked over me. 'Didn't take you long, did it?' His eyes were on my chest, which has become something of an explosion lately. 'It suits you. I think I'll take you somewhere so we can see how much.' I shouted at him to let me go and he just laughed at me. 'Or what? You will call your doctor boyfriend on me?'

I said yes, that Mattaus would make sure his superiors knew how he was pestering me.

Which was when he laughed and pointed at a new emblem on his shirt. 'Superiors? See that? That means I am now a major.'

'So?' I said.

His eyes glittered. 'It means that dear old Herr Fredericks has to answer to me now…'

I felt myself pale at that. When I got home I told Mattaus, though he wasn't worried about Kroeling's promotion, just my run-in with him. He told me that the printing press they used to run out of the bookshop has grown larger so it doesn't make sense to bring it back here, and with Kroeling's advanced duties it means he is now more involved in checking things like the borders, and arranging other issues. One of those, I hate to say, has to do with the Jews. News has reached us that they have started rounding them up and taking them to internment camps. Papa told me that one of the people who were taken was our old piano teacher, Madame Avril. How I cried when I heard. I begged Mattaus to do something – but what can one man do? It's the most awful, hateful thing. I despise myself for being so pathetically grateful that you are safe, or at least I hope you are… when I know they are not. I hate this war and these Nazis… and what they have done to us all.

M was sick when he heard about what they have done. It turns out his grandfather was Jewish. I heard him retching in the night. I know he knows more than he tells me. I wonder if he feels so ill because he worries they will find out about his grandfather, or because the people he grew up with are capable of such monstrous things. Perhaps it is both…

Valerie set down the stack of letters, and put them beneath a pile of paperwork on her bistro desk as Dupont shuffled into the bookshop.

She looked at the old man – there were so many questions she had for him. So many things she wanted – needed – to understand. She opened her mouth – heart racing – as she prepared to speak the words she had kept from him for so long. The secret she needed to share. She cleared her throat and he looked at her with a frown. 'Did you take a bath in your coffee today?' he asked, looking at her with a frown, his lips amused.

She looked down and saw that all over her white top were dark coffee dribbles. By the time she had looked up again, the moment had passed, and all she felt as she went upstairs to change, the letters clutched beneath her arm, was bone tired.

CHAPTER TWENTY-SEVEN

A week later, to her shock, Valerie discovered something she had in common with her mother.

She was pregnant. Or at least, she might be. She looked at her small school diary, in which she wrote things like 'ten a.m., hair appointment', and frowned as she paged back through the past several weeks to the last time she had written a little red X for her period.

She put her head in her hands. She was smarter than this – or at least, so she'd thought. She and Freddy had used protection. Except, well… maybe not always, she realised with mounting dread. She thought back to a drunken evening a few weeks ago when Freddy had run out of condoms and she had blithely, drunkenly declared, 'What harm will just the once do…'

Oh. Good. God, she thought now. While the fact that she and Freddy loved each other gave her some comfort, this was not how she would have pictured this happening… with her sleeping in a tiny child's bed pretending to be somebody named Isabelle Henry, and with Freddy renting the world's worst garret.

When she stood up, she felt the world spin, and ran to the toilet to be sick, hoping it wasn't the start of morning sickness.

Later that evening, while Dupont was out doing some shopping, she made herself a cup of tea and sat reading the baby book in the kitchen, planning to put it back where she'd found it afterwards.

But she found herself looking at it more and more. It suddenly meant even more to her with her current fears. She didn't hear Dupont come into the kitchen – so engrossed was she that she startled when he touched her shoulder. She made to hide the book, looking shiftily from it to Dupont, but she could tell by his expression that he had already seen. His face had grown pale, and she momentarily lost the power of speech.

'I – M'sieur Dupont – I am sorry. I found it by the cook-books…' She could have kicked herself for reading it in here – if she'd kept it in her room he never would have known.

A muscle flexed in his jaw, and he snapped it up from the table and shoved it under his arm. His blue eyes were intense with anger, and she looked down, swallowing.

'So you thought you would just *read it* – even though it was someone's private possession.'

Valerie closed her eyes, shame flooding her cheeks. 'I – I shouldn't have, I apologise.'

His face was livid. He opened his mouth, then shut it again. She could tell that it was taking a lot for him to keep his calm. For someone as hot-blooded as he could be, this made her feel worse, made her feel the gravity of his disappointment. He took a deep breath and said, 'I shouldn't have left it here if I didn't want it read.'

Then he turned and walked out. She saw on the table the string bag from the supermarket, filled with tea bags, scones, a pot of strawberry jam and cream, and felt terrible. He had obviously been thinking of her when he went to the shops, which only made it worse. He had been doing a lot of that lately, getting English things for her – it seemed so out of character, and sweet, and it made her feel truly awful for hurting him now.

She followed him to the living room, where he had settled with the evening's newspaper, a cigarette between his lips, a deep frown between his eyes. He was literally hiding behind the pages.

When she tried to discuss the baby book with him, he told her to just leave it alone. 'It's forgotten, leave it be.' His tone was cool; his manner said *drop it.*

But still she could tell he couldn't. The following day there was tension between them all day, and Valerie began to worry that if this was how he would take her just looking at her mother's things, how was he going to take the news that she was the grandchild he had given away – returned now to live here in secret?

She sighed, and went for a walk, ending up at Freddy's. There was so much she had to tell him – starting with the news that she was possibly pregnant, but she kept that to herself for now. She would tell him when she knew for sure, she decided. So she told him what had happened. About the baby book.

He was sitting on the mattress, the green typewriter on his lap. His shirt was unbuttoned. 'A book of your first months? Wow.'

She nodded. Wow indeed. 'It was… I don't know how to explain, aside from wonderful, mostly, to find it. It's not big – I mean, the entries are just little observations, sentences scattered through various weeks, but here and there, it's a record of a mother's love, and knowing it was about me, I…'

She bit her lip, and felt the tears start to form. 'It just makes it so real. What was taken from me – *who* was taken from me during this war. I would have loved to have known her.'

Freddy reached out for her. 'Oh, love. I'm so sorry.'

She nodded, took a shaky breath, then wiped the tears from her eyes. 'It also makes a lot of this worth it too, you know, because in a way I have found her again. Madame Joubert gave me these letters she wrote her, too – and while some of it is a bit hard to digest, and there's a part of me that knows if I had never come here, I could have been spared the truth about where I come from – I might never have known her at all. And that sort of makes all of this worth it in the end.'

When she got home later that night she found Dupont sitting in the living room, a bottle of pale yellow coloured liquor before him, as he sat staring at the baby book.

Valerie bit her lip as she walked in. He looked up, and nodded at her in greeting. 'Come, sit,' he said. 'Can I pour you a glass of pastis?'

'Pastis?'

'It's made from aniseed. It's very good, from Provence.'

She nodded. 'All right.'

She sipped the liquor, and pulled a face. It tasted like liquorice.

The baby book was lying open next to him, but he didn't bring it up. He asked her about her evening, and how Freddy was. She realised that he felt bad for how he'd snapped, but he wasn't going to open up to her about the book. She knew that she was going to have to be the one who did it.

'She loved the baby very much,' she said, indicating the book.

Dupont's eyes grew dark, and he closed it suddenly, standing up. 'I think it's time for me to go to bed.'

'No, wait, M'sieur. I'm sorry.'

He closed his eyes. 'I don't want to talk about this. Please, excuse me.'

'No.'

He turned to look at her, surprise on his lined face. His cotton-wool hair stuck up from where he'd been sitting against the sofa.

'No?'

She took a deep, steadying breath, and stood up as well. 'No, we have to talk about this.'

He blinked at her – perhaps at the audacity of her ordering him about in his own house. He was on the verge of saying so when she held up a hand. Then she reached inside her handbag and took out the photograph of her mother that she'd put in there that morning, the one from her suitcase, which she'd had since she was a little girl. Her hands shook as she passed it to him.

He stared at it for some time in confusion. Then he looked up at her, and seemed to stagger.

She caught his arm, steadying him.

He held out a hand to the wall, and said faintly, 'Where did you get this?'

His eyes were fierce, and so very blue.

Valerie's heart was thundering so loud in her ears she was afraid he could hear it.

She swallowed, and told him truthfully, 'I have always had it, since I was a baby. It was the only picture I have ever had of my mother.'

She had to help him sit down when his knees gave way.

'Y-you are – you are…' It was as if he wouldn't dare say it aloud.

'I am Valerie Dupont.'

Dupont stared at her in shock. 'Valerie,' he said, then said it again. 'Valerie.' And his face crumpled, and the old man began to sob in a way that broke Valerie's heart.

He let her touch his back, and she sat in mortified silence as his shoulders shook, the tears unable to stop coursing down his old, worn cheeks.

After a while, when he had at last gathered his composure, she poured him another glass of pastis not realising that the reason she couldn't see him properly to hand it over was because tears were slipping down her own face.

'How is this even possible?' he breathed, after some time.

So she explained, about everything. It was a long story, but to her surprise when she mentioned the advertisement he actually laughed, looking up at her through red-rimmed eyes. 'So you lied about that paper to make sure I hired you,' he snorted, shaking his head. 'It worked too.'

She grinned as she nodded. Her hands shook as she took a sip of the pastis she had poured herself, then put it quickly back down on the table as she remembered that she probably shouldn't be drinking. 'You aren't angry?'

He looked up at her in surprise. 'Angry, with you?'

Another tear fell from his eye, and his chin wobbled. He picked up his glass, though it just shook in his hands. 'My dear, the only one here who has any right to be angry is you.'

All her secrets came pouring out then. Everything Madame Joubert had told her. Everything she had since managed to find out. Dupont was outraged that Madame Joubert had kept this from him. 'When I see her – I am going to give her hell.'

'Don't, I think she has had enough…'

He wiped his nose, lit a cigarette and nodded, the fight seeming to evaporate just as suddenly from him. 'In that you may be right.'

She made them tea – and the scones he'd bought earlier, which he, in a very un-Dupont-like way, declared were delicious. Halfway through his second bite she could see that he had begun to weep again. She came to sit next to him, and held his hand. To her surprise he held on tightly to hers, then shook his head. 'I am an old man, *chérie*, but you have made me very happy today. I never imagined… this. That I would get to meet you, to discover that the young girl I had come to think of a little like a daughter, was in fact… you. I would have thought that I suddenly believed in fairy tales and second chances, and I have never been accused of either' – he squeezed her hand, and sniffed – 'till now.'

CHAPTER TWENTY-EIGHT

Dupont and Valerie walked to the Jardin des Tuileries, and sat at a restaurant overlooking the winter garden.

They had been slightly awkward with each other that morning at breakfast, being overly polite after the emotions that had come pouring out the night before. But soon after the first cup of coffee, and the decision – the first in decades – to close the Gribouiller on a Saturday was made, they decided to get out, to walk and to talk.

There was so much he wanted to know. 'What was your house like – was it a house?'

'Yes.' She nodded. 'It was a terraced house, in north London. Standard issue, two up two down.'

'What is this "standard issue"?' he asked. So she had to explain English housing, and suburban living in general.

'*C'est fou,*' he exclaimed. Then: 'Go on.'

So she did. She told him about Amélie. And her uncle, John, who had been like a father to her. He had taught her how to ride a bike. Encouraged her love of reading…

At this Dupont scoffed and said categorically that this must have been in her blood, what with the bookshop, and she admitted that there was a good chance of that.

When they were sitting down at the restaurant, though, she opened up her bag and took out the old copy of *The Secret Garden* that she had brought with her from England.

Dupont's eyes widened when she passed it to him. His fingers touched the faint G stamped on the endpaper. He tapped it, shaking his head, his eyes watering slightly. 'For Gribouiller,' he said, and there were tears in her eyes too at the discovery.

'I put it in the suitcase… that day,' said Dupont, referring to the day when Amélie had come to take her away to England.

Valerie stared at it.

'I wanted you to have something of hers, something to treasure, along with the photograph.'

She closed her eyes, taking a steadying breath. 'I did. All this time. But it was only the other day – when we were in the shop, when you told me that it had been her favourite book – that I realised that it had come from here.'

'She would have been so happy that you loved it as she did.'

As the sun began to wane, and they walked back along the river, he told her how despite her fears, having a baby was the joy of Mireille's young life.

CHAPTER TWENTY-NINE

1942

All her fears of giving birth, and of how people would react on the streets to the news that she had a baby by a German officer, melted away during those twilight weeks that followed Valerie's birth. The apartment became a cocoon where only they existed.

Mireille and the baby.

Mattaus was there as often as he could get away from his work at the hospital, and her father came up often in the day, but for the most part it was the two of them in their little world, which had grown smaller, yet somehow richer.

She named the baby Valerie after her mother, who had died when she was nine from pneumonia. Yet somehow, stamped on her face, were her mother's lips, her ears, her nose.

She stared in wonder at her for hours. The fat little arms and chubby legs, the small squidgy feet that sat perfectly in the palms of her hands, like pearls.

Even her father fell under Valerie's spell. The wedge that had existed between them since he'd come home from jail, only to find that Mattaus had become more than just the bodyguard he'd hoped for, seemed to melt away too, as he held his granddaughter for the first time. When the child first appeared to smile, he swore it was just for him, even though Mireille hadn't the heart to tell him it was too early, and it was probably wind.

Soon Mireille's life revolved around a comfortable routine. She slept when Valerie slept, and she was proud to identify every cry – *wet, thirsty, windy, hungry, tired, bored.* The last one had taken a while for her to figure out, but when she took the baby to another, less frequented room and she saw how her daughter's eyes stared almost in wonder at the patterned wallpaper behind her, and the tears finally stopped, she realised that the time to go outside had arrived.

She was nervous as she put Valerie into the perambulator that Mattaus had brought home one evening, shortly after Valerie's birth. The device, or at least its predecessor, had been the cause of one of their first serious arguments. It was the latest model, shiny and new. It was obvious to anyone looking at it what type of person would be able to afford it in times like these – someone who had no doubt collaborated a bit more with the Germans than was approved of. Mattaus had stood firm, despite her protests; he wanted his child to have it. What did it matter what other people thought?

'Nothing,' Mireille had snapped. 'It's what they do with those thoughts that matters. I've seen some women shove and kick those children.' Her voice broke as she remembered the woman who had lost her baby when a mob had turned on her after the student riots. It was her greatest fear.

'They would never do that in front of me,' he said.

She looked at him in disbelief. 'And you can be sure to be around every moment to prevent it?'

His silence meant that she had struck a nerve. After some time, with less heat, he replied, 'Why do people have to be so cruel?'

Mireille sighed. It pained her how much she understood it, how part of her still twisted in shame, even though she knew that

Mattaus wasn't the enemy, wasn't like the others. 'For them it's a badge – their integrity, it's the only thing they have left. They polish it, like a stone, and throw it at others at will.'

Mattaus didn't speak about it with her again after that. But when he came home later that evening, the shiny new perambulator was gone, and in its place was an old, slightly rusted pram, dating from before the war. She kissed his cheek in gratitude. It was perfect.

But that was then.

She hadn't worked up the courage to actually use it, till now.

She drew in a deep breath as she pushed the pram away from the back door and started down the street, a small blossom of fear constricting her throat. She was waiting… waiting for someone she knew to walk past and spit on her, to call her names. To shake the pram. But, blessedly, the street was quiet, with very few people milling about. With the new rations imposed, she realised most people were conserving as much energy as they could.

She breathed a sigh of relief when they entered a park that ran along the Seine, and for a short while, in the streets of Paris, she was like any other young mother.

After that first day, it became their habit every day to visit the park. Mireille showed Valerie the ducks swimming in the river. Before the war, people would be throwing stale bread out to feed them, but those days were gone. You could still feed yourself on stale bread.

As she pushed the pram, she could, for a moment, though, imagine that they were no longer at war, no longer going through the Occupation.

Back at the bookshop, it was another matter entirely. Despite the Germans' best efforts to show that their Occupation was business as usual, and how well they were doing in the war, the truth was coming out in dark, dangerous whispers. The allies were a threat they couldn't suppress.

In secret, Vincent tuned in to an old transistor radio, listening to an illegal broadcast from the resistance. The man that Clotilde had mentioned, Charles de Gaulle, spoke of a recent uprising. They were told to keep going, to keep resisting. 'The time will come for us,' he promised.

Mattaus was unhappy when he found out that they were listening to the radio. He worried that if any of the neighbours turned them in they could pay for it with their lives.

Vincent was furious at the warning. To him, this proved once and for all that the man was a Nazi in his soul.

'It's the only protection we have – the illusion that I am who I say I am,' Mattaus attempted to explain. 'Anything else means that this will all come down like a stack of cards.'

Vincent sniffed. 'Are you sure that it is just an illusion?'

CHAPTER THIRTY

The uprising of the students who had marched against the Germans made headlines worldwide. But all too soon, after the leaders of the illegal protest were arrested, the rumours began. Mattaus came home with a grim set to his mouth. 'They are talking about making an example of them.'

Mireille looked up from where she was wiping spittle from the baby's mouth. 'You mean they will be sent to jail?'

'For now.'

She frowned. 'Surely they won't kill them just for a protest march?'

Mattaus looked at her in disbelief. 'Every day here people get shot for less.'

It was true. Times had got even tougher. And with winter fast approaching, along with Valerie's first birthday the following spring, the feeling on the streets of Paris was ever more grim. The Germans, it seemed, had stopped pretending to play nice.

Early at the start of the next year, the five student protesters were shot, execution style. When Vincent tuned in to the radio that night to hear, Mireille sneaked into his room. 'He won't be happy,' he warned.

But Mireille shrugged. 'I need to know what they are planning…' She cradled Valerie to her chest; she'd finally gone to sleep. 'I need to know that there is some future that my child can look forward to – an end to this never-ending war.'

The one thing that had improved over the past year was that, as Mattaus had predicted, they had seen less and less of Valter Kroeling. With his new promotion he hardly had the opportunity to come to the bookshop these days. A dour-faced man appointed with a thin salt and pepper moustache now came to inspect their stock and orders, and to ensure that they were not selling or distributing any banned books or material. Henrik Winkler did the task efficiently and left just as promptly.

After the uprising by the student protestors, the resistance had grown, and one of the women from Clotilde's old network, Thérèse Castelle, began to make contact with Mireille again when she noticed that Valter Kroeling was no longer at the bookshop as often. Mireille sensed that the woman, with her mouse-coloured hair and red scarf, who popped into the shop regularly, was attempting to see where Mireille's loyalties lay: with her German lover – no one had been told about their marriage, which would have been frowned upon by both the French and German authorities – or her own people.

Mireille suspected that Clotilde had told them of what she had done. She was passed a note one day by Thérèse, and when she opened it, she read: *Find out if it's true. Is the Fanatic coming to visit? If so, when? We need to prepare.*

Mireille burnt the note, her heart jackhammering in her chest. The Fanatic, she knew, meant the Führer – Hitler himself. He'd come for a day at the start of the Occupation, a victors' march through the streets of Paris, and there were many who wished that they had known where he was going to march, as they could have staged a shooting. It had been kept a secret then. But now, if he was coming back…

Mireille didn't know how the woman thought she could find out such a thing. But a few days later, the same woman came past and left another note, and she understood. *K is overseeing the event. If he says anything, let us know.*

It was part of Kroeling's new role, she realised. It made sense, she supposed: he was high up in the Nazi propaganda machine, and would no doubt know when Hitler was planning on coming, and when – and would be covering it for his magazine.

Which meant that she would need to ensure that he came to the shop himself – instead of Henrik Winkler. In order to do that she would need to draw him in.

He came a week later. His watery eyes were alight. 'Where is the table, Mademoiselle?'

'What table?' she asked, feigning innocence.

The muscle in his cheek flexed. 'The one in which we display our communications, as you well know. Our agreement was that it would remain here in the shop. It is the only reason you have been allowed to keep this... business,' he said, his eyes falling on the half-empty shelves. Vincent made to get out of his chair, but she shook her head at him, and he sat back down, Valerie cradled on his lap.

Kroeling's eye fell on the baby, and he snorted. 'Look how tenderly he cradles that German brat. We should take a photograph and show it to the Führer, the success of the Occupation – the German and French living so peacefully and happily together... the new generation dawning...'

Vincent's face went red with anger. But Mireille seized the opportunity. 'Does someone of your stature ever get the chance to speak to him? I wouldn't have thought so,' she needled.

As she'd hoped, he bristled. 'Yes, of course I do. I am key to this whole Occupation. He is very interested in what I have to say of its success.'

'But surely he is too busy, and won't take much notice of what is happening here when he is distracted by the fighting elsewhere…'

He scoffed, raising a hand in dismissal. 'The war is over – we have won. His efforts are now about keeping his people happy. Especially the people who are now under his command. Paris is the jewel in his empire, and he takes a keen interest in it, of course. It's why he is coming next week…'

'He is?'

'Yes. A victory march through the streets of Paris, starting with the Arc de Triomphe, of course, like Napoleon.'

'Of course,' said Mireille.

When Thérèse came two days later, Mireille placed the note in a novel by Alexandre Dumas, and handed it to her. 'Here is the novel you ordered.'

Inside it she had written: *Next week, Arc de Triomphe.*

The message of warning came the following day, from the man who ran the bakery around the corner: *Don't trust the old network.*

Mireille's throat turned dry. She thought about the drop. The woman with the red scarf. What had she done?

They came for Mireille on Valerie's first birthday. They had spent it at the park, at her favourite place, near the ducks. It was a small affair. Mireille had made a cake, saving the sugar from their tea for the week, and there was even a bit of pink icing. It was just the four of them on a picnic blanket, and for a while there in the early spring sunshine, Mireille could convince herself that she had nothing to fear – until they heard the sound of booted feet marching towards them. She looked up to find several brown-shirted officers coming at them, and her heart stuttered in sudden cold fear. They were led by Valter Kroeling, who fairly flew towards her, his watery blue eyes lit up as if there were a cool fire glowing inside him. Next to him was the woman in the red scarf, the one Mireille had passed the note about where and when Hitler would be arriving. She felt herself go pale. She understood at once. She was holding on to Valerie tighter than was necessary, and the child began to cry.

'What is the meaning of this?' asked Mattaus, standing up.

Kroeling turned to him, his brow quirked. 'I should be asking you that question, Herr Fredericks.'

He looked at the woman to his left, who was finding it hard to meet Mireille's eyes. 'This is the woman, you are sure?' he said to her. The woman didn't say anything and Kroeling barked, 'Thérèse Castelle, may I remind you what is at stake should you not answer.'

The woman raised her chin, tears leaking down her face, as she pointed at Mireille. '*Yes*. It was her.'

Valter Kroeling nodded, pursing his lips. His fingers reached inside his pocket, and took out a folded-up piece of paper. He handed the note to Henrik Winkler, who looked at it for a moment, then nodded. 'Arc de Triomphe, *oui*. Exactly as was planted…'

Valter Kroeling then gave Mireille a reluctant smile, though she could see the glee that was hidden behind it. 'Mireille Dupont, I am afraid our time had come to an end. You are accused of treason, against the Führer himself. Passing on messages about where he will be – a fabrication, *of course*,' he said, allowing himself a small smile. 'The Führer has no such plans to come back to Paris. He did his victory lap once – no need to keep coming back, when he has other territories to conquer. In that you were quite correct. But still, you fell for the bait, and for that I am afraid the sentence is death.'

'This is outrageous,' said Mattaus. 'What are you talking about? Treason against Hitler himself? This is some mad scheme of yours… you have been after her for ages, and now you've gone completely mad. I will not let you get away with this.'

Valter Kroeling gave a soft laugh. He had been waiting for this moment for a long time, Mireille realised, and he was enjoying it, now that it had finally arrived. 'I am a patient man, Herr Fredericks, and we have given your *wife* as much leeway as possible, but when information came our way that she was in fact sending messages to a scatty group of people who call themselves the resistance' – his hand fluttered towards Thérèse Castelle as he gave a small, derisive snort – 'we had to pay closer attention. It seems this has been going on for some time, beneath your nose.'

He brandished the note, which had Mireille's handwriting on it.

'This is her handwriting, is it not?'

When Mattaus didn't respond, Kroeling sighed. 'It makes no difference, I'm afraid. It's a very clear case.'

The air left Mireille's lungs.

He clicked his fingers, and one of the men came forward to seize her, ripping the baby out of her arms. Valerie began to howl, as if somehow she sensed that this was the last time she would ever see her mother, ever feel the touch of her embrace.

The baby was given over to Dupont, who rushed forward to take her.

'You can't do this,' he said.

Kroeling looked at him, enjoying hurting the man who had once dared to strike him. 'It has already been done.'

Then he looked at Mattaus and said, 'Alas, I do not like to see two people so *in love* separated, so you will be arrested as well, Herr Fredericks, as you are responsible for your wife's actions, and have been seen to be complicit. We have this here,' he said, reaching inside his jacket pocket and brandishing another folded-up piece of paper. 'This is a confession from the priest who married you. It seems you kept this information from your superiors. It has since been decided that if you could keep your very marriage a secret, there is no telling what else you are hiding. The sentence for you is, of course… death by firing squad. If you're lucky we can arrange that the two of you go together.'

Mattaus's eyes flashed with fury and fear. 'You will not be taking me or my wife anywhere.'

'Accept it, Fredericks. It's over.'

Another man came forward to seize Mattaus. There was a struggle, and the soldier went down as Mattaus struck him with an elbow to the nose. Valter Kroeling drew his pistol, but Mattaus had already seized the gun of the downed soldier, and the blast went off like an explosion. Kroeling doubled over, screaming, his hands cupping a seeping wound in his side, his face turning ashen. In the next moment two shots were fired, and seemingly, as if in slow motion, Dupont watched as Mireille slumped over, sliding ever so slowly to the ground. She landed on her knees, then fell, her arms still reaching for her child. Mattaus blinked as he stared at his wife. He screamed her name, but no sound seemed to come out. His hand came up to touch his heart, which had begun to explode in pain, and as he touched his chest, he felt the warm flow of blood. When he looked up he saw the pistol still smoking in Kroeling's dead hand.

He staggered to Mireille, touched her face, and lay down next to her. The last thing he saw before he died was her face.

CHAPTER THIRTY-ONE

1963

'She was betrayed,' said Valerie at last. They had been sitting on a bench where they'd come to a stop just along the Rue des Oiseaux. She'd sunk down onto it as Dupont began to tell her about the day her parents had died. There was a moment when she hadn't wanted to hear any more, when she wanted him to stop, but a part of her needed to know, needed to understand what had happened.

'She died for nothing,' she said, staring at the ground. 'She risked everything… and it was all just a set-up.'

She wanted to rage, to scream. To find Valter Kroeling's remains and tear them apart.

Dupont grabbed her hand and squeezed it. 'No, not for nothing. She was fooled, yes, but had it been true, she could have changed the fate of the war. We don't know, when we take a chance, when we decide to do the right thing, if it will work or not – we just have to take the leap, do what is asked of us. She was brave, and that can never be taken away from her. That's how we won the war, in the end. By taking those chances. As your father did when he saved Clotilde. He could have been killed if they had found out.'

She nodded, and dashed the tears from her eyes. She supposed he had thought about this for a long time. She knew, as well, that her mother would have been gratified to hear that so many years after her husband's death, her father did think that Mattaus was brave and good… she had got that wish at least, in the end.

They walked on together, back to the bookshop, back home.

CHAPTER THIRTY-TWO

'You're pregnant?'

Valerie nodded. She was sitting across from Freddy at the Cafe De Bonne Chance. Jazz music was playing, and in the corner, a beautiful woman with long brown hair was laughing.

'Are you sure?'

'I think so… I'm very late.'

Freddy stared at her, his brown eyes wide. His fingers went to play with the back of his hair. 'Shit.'

She made a small noise. This was not how she had pictured it. She closed her eyes. She had been a smart girl, once. Before she ran away to Paris pretending to be Isabelle Henry.

'That's great, thanks, Freddy.'

He laughed. 'Val.'

She folded her arms. 'Look, I'm not exactly thrilled either, but…' He was still grinning at her, so she snapped, 'What?'

'Well, I…' He shifted in his seat. 'I saw this at the pawn shop around the corner today. I mean, it's not flashy or anything, and I bought it because, I don't know, it just seemed right… I had hoped to wait a bit, till I had an apartment… and definitely before you said *that*.'

'What are you talking about?' said Valerie, who hadn't really been paying attention past him saying 'shit' at the news that she was pregnant. Even if, admittedly, it *was* rather *shit* in terms of timing, but… a baby, well, it could be…

'Val?'

She looked up and blinked. There was a ring. A flash of something that sparkled.

'I mean, I'll get you a better one when I actually make us some money… but… will you marry me?'

'Oh, Jesus, Freddy,' she said, and then she burst into tears. It was perhaps the worst proposal but one of the most romantic moments of her life, second only to the day he'd told her that he loved her.

When she got home later that evening, she found Madame Joubert sitting upstairs with Dupont. When she came inside, the conversation stopped. She took a seat next to Madame Joubert, and said, 'Well, I suppose now everyone knows.'

'Yes,' Madame Joubert said, and she shook her head, her eyes wide. 'Can I pour you some wine?'

Valerie blew out her cheeks, then shook her head. 'I can't drink… not for the next nine months, I'm afraid.'

Both of their mouths fell open.

Madame Joubert gasped. 'You are…?'

Valerie nodded. 'Pregnant. Yes. Also' – she raised her hand – 'engaged.'

Madame Joubert screeched in excitement, and then she pulled Valerie into a tight hug, and the two of them started speaking excitedly about weddings and flowers. Valerie told her how upset Freddy was that he hadn't popped the question before, because now everyone would think that they were getting married only because she was pregnant. But her real concern was the garret. 'At the moment we can't really afford anything else. Rents in Paris aren't cheap, and Freddy is only freelancing. But hopefully he can get a permanent placement soon.'

'Here, do you think, or in England?' asked Madame Joubert.

'I'm not sure. Here, hopefully. Maybe England. I suppose that makes more sense, though… I don't know. We haven't yet decided.'

After some time Dupont stood up. His face looked downcast, though he said, 'I wish you all the best, truly. It is happy news.'

She watched him shuffle off down the passage to his bedroom, a frown on his face, his shoulders even more stooped than usual.

She turned back to Madame Joubert and asked, 'Is he all right?'

'Yes, it's just been a lot to take in, I'm sure.'

Valerie nodded. Yes, that made sense. She couldn't understand why he looked sad though, all of a sudden – he'd seemed so happy before.

'What happened when you came back from Spain? How did you end up living here again?' asked Valerie that night. It was a question she'd been dying to know the answer to – Clotilde's story, and how she had come back to Paris after the war.

Madame Joubert took a sip of her wine, and Valerie was swept back into the past.

Clotilde had been living in the Spanish mountains for three years, in a small village with other refugees. She was safe, she was free, and she was miserable too. She missed Paris. The streets, the gentle undulation of the Seine, the way the light turned from gold to rose as it reflected off the buildings in the afternoon. It was home. But what she longed for was a place that was no more.

News of Mireille's death had reached her, at last, through an old friend, a homosexual clockmaker named Michel Biomme, who the year before had crossed the border over the Alps with only the clothes on his back. When they saw each other, she saw in his eyes straight away that the news from home was bad. Clotilde and Mireille had been friends since they were babes, and for a long time after Clotilde heard of Mireille's death, she felt as if she couldn't breathe. It felt almost too cruel to contemplate that the two people who had sacrificed so much to ensure her own safety were gone, while she was here.

As the days passed she thought over the other things Michel had told her.

That there was a child, named Valerie. And that Monsieur Dupont had been left alone to care for her. He who had been the closest thing she'd ever had to a father. She needed to return to Paris for them.

'I would never return, never, not after what has happened,' said Jean, an older Jewish woman who had spent eight months in a labour camp before she escaped and ended up here in this small village called Hela, in the Spanish countryside. Jean and some of the others called it Hell for short due to the scant resources, and the government's inability to help them when there were so many others who were in the same boat.

'It wasn't their fault, what happened to us,' said Clotilde.

'Don't be naive,' spat Jean. 'It was my neighbour who told them where we were hiding in the attic. My *neighbour*, Clotilde. A man that I had known for twenty years. I had looked after his children when they were ill. Had cooked for them, sent over gifts at Christmas – for Christmas,' she emphasised. The holiday they did not celebrate. 'And still, in the end, he decided that he would rather earn a quick buck from the Germans than protect us. I wouldn't go back there if you paid me.'

A lot of the others felt the same: betrayed by their own people. Some, like Clotilde, were more philosophical. There were others like her who had escaped due to the leniency and help of their enemy.

'People show who they are in war,' said Jean. This was true, thought Clotilde. Sometimes, like Mattaus, the good comes out; sometimes just the will to survive, to feed a family, never mind the cost to others.

Clotilde couldn't think about that, not now.

It took two weeks for her to travel back. She waited just long enough to hear that the war was well and truly over before she packed the small bag she'd arrived with, and made her way across the border.

The streets of Paris were filled with people. Allied soldiers were everywhere, smiles lighting their faces. In the streets, Charles de Gaulle's name was spoken often and with reverence. Everywhere there was a sense of triumph, of joy: it was finally over.

Clotilde paused before the bookshop. The glass was dirty, the gold lettering dull. It was closed, when it had never been closed on a Saturday for as long as she could remember.

She rang the bell, and it was some time before she heard footsteps, and found Dupont at the door.

His eyes widened when he saw her, then his head fell upon her broad shoulder, and he clasped her to him as a daughter. When they pulled apart, they took in the ravages that war had left behind. Dupont had aged dramatically: his hair had turned white, and his shoulders were beginning to stoop. He looked like an old man, though he was barely fifty-five. His eyes were haunted, lost.

'You didn't need to come,' he said.

'Yes, I did.'

Clotilde didn't want to hear about the rumours. About what was happening on the streets. It didn't mean anything, she insisted, but Dupont was adamant. 'They are calling it a purge, Clotilde. Lisette Minoutte was shot, just for helping a woman who'd slept with a German to give birth. She was a trained midwife, for goodness' sake, and it was her neighbour. What will they do to the children?'

Already some of the children were being shunned by their families. Dupont had heard of one child who'd been so badly beaten that he had to be taken to the hospital. It was not what he wanted for Valerie.

Clotilde was too late. By just one day. Amélie had already come to fetch the child by the time Clotilde had arrived.

They'd had to do it in secret. Because the French were drawing up the names of all the collaborators, and no one was sure their children wouldn't end up on those lists – to be sent somewhere else, somewhere far away.

Dupont had made Amélie promise not to tell him where she moved to – so that he couldn't follow.

Madame Joubert looked at Valerie now. 'I was devastated. If I had arrived sooner, maybe I could have raised you myself, pretended you were my own… but it was too late, and we didn't know where to start. We convinced ourselves that you would have a good life with Amélie. It was all we had left to cling to. I hope you can forgive me.'

Valerie took her hand. She bit her lip, tears falling down her face as she realised, 'You came back for me.'

She nodded.

CHAPTER THIRTY-THREE

The bookshop cat was curled up on her desk, and Valerie sat up to shift her weight. She was uncomfortable, no matter which way she sat. Her pregnancy had started to show, and her feet were like two ham sandwiches in her rather unflattering men's sandals. But still, she wasn't about to let Dupont get away with his last retort.

'Are you actually joking? You can't throw someone out of the shop just because they don't like *A Tale of Two Cities*.'

'Yes, I can.'

'No, you can't.'

Freddy's voice cut through: 'I found it sentimental. I'm sorry, M'sieur.'

She could tell he was enjoying this. Privately she was a little worried that the two of them would actually end up killing each other… now that Freddy had moved in.

In the end, after two weeks of morose, taciturn silence following the news that she was pregnant and that she and Freddy were to be married, Madame Joubert had had enough. It was she who suggested to Dupont that he offer to have Valerie and Freddy come to live here, with him.

Valerie had looked up at Madame Joubert, and stuttered, 'Madame… I think M'sieur Dupont wouldn't want to have us all here intruding on him…'

Her grandfather was staring at her with a strange expression on his face.

'Don't you want to live with him?' asked Madame Joubert. 'Don't you enjoy working here, living in Paris?' She took a drag of her cigarette, her kohl-rimmed eyes wide, probing.

'Of course I do, I *love* it here. But still, it's *a lot* to ask and I don't want to be a burden.'

'Pah!' exploded Dupont. They each turned to look at him. 'What burden? I have room, I like working with you. Besides, I can't bear the idea of you in that fleapit garret in Montmartre with my great-grandchild…' He shuddered, then slowly started to smile.

'Really?' said Valerie, her eyes widening, hope filling her chest at the possibility. Everything she'd said was true. She really did love it here, and she wasn't ready to move back to England – not yet, anyway.

He looked at her, and then at Madame Joubert. His expression contained something she didn't recognise at first, and then she knew. It was gratitude. It was why he'd been so morose these past few weeks, she realised, and it touched her more than she could bear. He'd thought she was going to *leave*.

She stood up and gave him a hug, and whispered, 'Perhaps it's time we both started believing in second chances and happy endings.'

There were tears in his eyes as he nodded. Then he kissed the top of her head, and it was a long time before he let her go.

CHAPTER THIRTY-FOUR

Present day

The night had turned from pink and gold to deepest blue and smoky black. Through the window, they could see the stars come out as the loudspeaker announced that the next stop would be Paris.

Annie would have been surprised to note that there were tracks of mascara from her tears all down her face.

The old woman next to her had long since gone from being a stranger to a friend, as Valerie Lea-Sparrow shared her story.

Annie had got up to fetch Valerie's cobalt blue suitcase, which she'd helped stow only a few hours before, and watched as Valerie opened it to reveal the things that she'd spoken about. The old novel, *The Secret Garden*, with the faded G stamped on the endpaper, now more than seventy years old. A picture of Freddy, handsome and boyish, with his tousled hair, cheeky grin, and a typewriter on his lap, a cigarette dangling between his teeth. There was even a photograph of Dupont at a messy desk, a boy with wild unruly hair sitting on his lap.

'What happened next?' asked Annie, wanting, needing to know how it had turned out.

Valerie looked at the last photograph tenderly, and said, 'Together we ran the Gribouiller until his death in eighty-four. Freddy and I lived in the apartment, and we raised our two children – a boy, whom we called Vincent, and a girl we called Mireille, after my mother. We moved back to England when he got a job as a producer for the BBC, but we kept the apartment – I have it still.

'Freddy died four years ago. He got an infection in his lungs, and was gone in such a short time, I could hardly prepare myself.' There were tears in Valerie's eyes, and Annie's too. 'But it was quick. He didn't suffer, which I suppose in the end was a blessing.'

As the train pulled into the station, the old woman stood up, wrapped a cashmere shawl around herself, and, with Annie's help, made her way out of the station. She looked at her reflection in the window, and for just a moment she saw a young girl with long blonde hair and a battered suitcase at her feet. She lifted her chin, and she remembered now, as she did then, what she had told herself: courage. That's all she needed now.

Two weeks later…

It was wedged between a bistro and a flower shop, a sliver of a shop on the Rue des Oiseaux, the street of the birds. She saw the faded gold lettering, and twisted the old brass knob. The shop bell tinkled and Annie walked inside. Her eyes marvelled at the overflowing shelves, the stacks of paperback towers on the floor, the big messy desk in the corner, complete with a black-and-white bookshop cat. She felt a mixture of excitement and nerves. She couldn't believe she was actually *here*. She wondered if her mother would be proud of her for finally doing something she had always said she'd like to do one day.

A beam of light fell from the open door, and onto the old woman sitting behind the desk. There was a cigar in her mouth, unlit, and as the bell tinkled, she looked up with a smile. The kind of smile that turned strangers into friends. She frowned, and then said,

'Annie?'

'Hello,' said Annie, a nervous smile about her lips as she stepped forward, held out a piece of paper. It had felt like a sign when she'd read it in *Le Monde* that morning. When she'd decided that perhaps, like a certain woman she'd come to know, courage and a new start in Paris was exactly what she needed. She bit her lip and said, 'I came about the position I saw advertised… for a *bookseller*.'

Valerie stared at her for some time, and then she stood up and let out a low, throaty laugh.

'I had this feeling, call me mad or old,' she said, shaking her head. Her eyes twinkled as she showed Annie up the stairs. 'The position doesn't pay very well, but there is a room, with a *kettle*.'

AUTHOR'S NOTE

This story was inspired by an article I read in the *Independent*, called 'France finally acknowledges its war children'.

In France, 200,000 children grew up as the offspring of German soldiers from the Occupation during the Second World War. When the war ended, the women from these relationships were treated as 'collaborators' and they were jailed, some executed, and humiliated by having their heads shaved and being paraded through the streets of Paris in front of crowds of angry mobs. The stigma of being born to one of these women and a German father ensured that, through no fault of their own, some of these children were stigmatised, ostracised and ridiculed. So much so that many of them, when they could, reached out to German relatives – and this is where some were welcomed.

The Occupation, however, was a story of a survival. The city of Paris was, in effect, abandoned by the government, and in many ways its women were left alone to defend themselves – some were raped and tortured, and many resisted. Some, yes, fell in love. Some slept with soldiers to improve the situation for themselves and their children. Through it all they tried to deal with a very unfair situation, and to survive.

I didn't set out to write a romance between a German officer and a Frenchwoman. Mattaus appeared, and I began to imagine what it would have looked like if an officer like him began to question the practices of his government, and what that might mean.

The main story, however, was born out of this question: what would a parent or grandparent do, if they knew that they might spare the child the pain of being ridiculed and ostracised for something over which they had no control?

I must note, however, that the Germans were not alone in fathering children in enemy territory. In fact, it is estimated that a quarter of a million children were fathered by allied soldiers to German mothers during the Second World War, and many of these children had no idea who their fathers were, and were stigmatised by their own community – even speaking about it, on both sides, remains a difficult subject. It is a fact that, as Valerie says at the beginning of the story, 'What so many men have failed to realise after waging all these wars is that there are no real victors – there are only casualties, and they keep coming long after the battle has passed.' For the children of these wars and the psychological scars they have endured, this remains true.

For the purposes of this story some of the events and the timescale were shifted slightly – such as the forced wearing of the Star of David, which didn't occur as quickly as it was portrayed in the novel. Also, the rank of a senior doctor, while technically a 'captain' in the Wehrmacht, would not have commanded a position of authority in the army outside the medical corps.

A LETTER FROM LILY

Thank you so much for reading *The Paris Secret*. I really hope you enjoyed it. Paris has always held a special place in my heart, and I have long been fascinated by its history, its light, darkness and beauty, and particularly its ability to withstand so much. If you enjoyed this story, I'd so appreciate it if you could leave a review; it really helps to spread the word! If you're wondering what's next, I'm busy working on my next novel, set in Devon, featuring a group of female friends during the Second World War, which should be out in 2019.

If you want to keep up-to-date with all my latest releases, just sign up at the following link. Your email address will never be shared and you can unsubscribe at any time.

www.bookouture.com/lily-graham

I love hearing from my readers – you can get in touch on my Facebook page, through Twitter, Goodreads or my website.

Thanks so much,
Lily

LilyRoseGrahamAuthor

@lilygrahambooks

www.lilygraham.net

ACKNOWLEDGEMENTS

Thanks as ever to my incredible editor, Lydia Vassar-Smith, whose insight and enthusiasm for this book made it such a joy to write. I couldn't do it without you.

Thanks to my husband, Rui, who is always patient and there with an action plan when I'm battling feelings of overwhelm and sure that the ability to write a novel has deserted me. To Mom and Dad, and the entire Bradley and Valente clan for all your love, support and encouragement.

Also to the fabulous Bookouture team – Kim Nash, Alexandra Holmes, Natalie Butlin and the rest of the brilliant gang for always going above and beyond.

Also thank you so much to my dear readers, who make this the best job in the world.

All mistakes are, of course, my own.